Stile 101

Don't Let the u

D0807181

A

Novel

By

Lenaise Meyeil

Precioustymes Entertainment

KN FEB 08

This book is a work of fiction. Names, characters, place and incidents are results of the author's imagination or are used fictitiously. Any resemblance to locations, actual events or persons, living or dead is entirely coincidental.

Precioustymes Entertainment
901 Governors Place, #138
Bear, DE 19701
precioustymesent@aol.com
www.precioustymes.com

Library of Congress Control Number: 2005903629
ISBN# 0-9729325-3-4
Editor: Joanie Smith
Cover Design/Graphics: www.ocjgraphix.com
Cover Models: Shenetta Giles (front) www.shenetta.com
Tronda (back) www.tronda.net
Front cover photo courtesy of: Ryan Nash
Back cover photo courtesy of: Maurice White

First Trade Paperback Edition Printing May 2005
Printed in the United States of America

Introduction and compilation copyrights © 2005 by Precioustymes Entertainment

Acknowledgements

First to the head of my life, all glory to God. Philippians: Chapter 4:13 – I can do all things through God, which strengths me.

Much love and appreciation to my mother, Linda Williams and to my big sister, Nakita Williams. Thanks for being my backbone as well as my crutch, and never judging me. Most importantly, never complaining even when I thought you two were my personal ATM. ☺ Nakiya, my niece, I love you girl and all that I do is for you, That look you give me that tells me you are proud and admire me, it inspires me! I don't want you to look at me in any other way; I love you more than life itself. Termaine, my little brother, thanks for putting up with my demanding ways and letting me think I'm the boss – even though you stand over me like a tree - we both know who would win the fight. ☺ To the Twins, Deonte "Deon" and Deandre "DJ", my little cousins, I love you like my little brothers. Keep up those good grades and I'll keep treating! Big cousin Kim "Cruella Daville", you know I love you girl with your evil ass, thanks for always allowing a disagreement to be just that. To my cousins Candis, Erica and Janta, regardless of what you've done that I haven't, I'm still your BIG COUSIN. Stay positive and always remember family is family. And, even if you traded us for a new one, you will still have to deal with family issues – that's natural – just know it's all love. Jabril and Jammal Hodges, I'm so proud of you two "College Boys." Tanya my road dog, my ace, girl you know we got stories for days, so the next book is on you. My two aunts, Carlita and Daneen, thanks for all the pep talks and support. Daneen don't read this out loud until you call Carlita on the 3-way and thanks for listening to my every problem and keeping me grounded. ☺ Grandma Betty thanks for all the love and not allowing the distance to separate us. Grandma Catharine, it's because of you I believe – *'If it doesn't kill me it will only make me stronger'* – you are my lady knight. Janea "JD-Padey," you still my favorite gurl, we're going to take that trip you long for – am I gon' teach you how to stunt ma'? ☺ Cuzo Omar, Uncle Johnny, Uncle Andre, Uncle Eric and young Unk Josh, you guys don't know how much your inspirational words mean to me thanks for the love. Skeet even though I grew out of my tomboy ways, I'm still rolling with you, I love you boy. Aunt DEE-DEE, Uncle Lenny, Doshell "Dodie", big cuz Kenny, Ryan, Robert and Yosheda, thanks for the love and support. To all of my little cousins, its so many of you, but you all should know Meno love the kids, always remember the sky is the limit. Mary Isabel "Granny", thanks for making me feel like apart of the Kintop/Isabell family, and always letting me know if I need you, you're there without question, I love you for that. To all of my brothers and sisters, I bet y'all thought I forgot about you, Cresha wouldn't let that one slide. ☺ I never considered any of you my half siblings… we are blood! Tavaria, Maraino, Chris, Evalisha, Lacresha, Lil Otis, Shalonda "Pooh", and Morgan. Daddy was doing his thang, but one thing about it, he produced nothing but Quality. I love y'all. To all my nieces, and nephews, *Auntie* loves y'all. Burnadean Jackson thanks for being my second mom; you never treated me any way less than a daughter, thanks Ma.

For my extended family, Aunt Charmaine, Shelia "Tasharma", Tony, Bo, Brittany, it's all love FAM. Danise

Word, one remark for you "unforgettable", much love to you and lil cuz Crystal "light light," I'm so proud of you girl, we all have a bond that nobody will ever understand. Marquwida Winters, it's time gurl, *Shine, Shine, Shine!!* And to the Darby family, you know who you are, the love goes way back to ding, dong ditch.☺ We have a life long attachment. To *"Our Way Entertainment,"* I look forward to that 'free' book release party!! *(Just kidding) J'm putting you on front street Lydell.*

To my girls, the real *"Classy Clique"*, Lakesha Kintop, Patrice Dickerson, Zakesha Hamilton, Jackie Mosby, Camesha Johnson-Lewis and our extended members Marquisia Melton, Valeria Hamilton and Kesha Arnold. Y'all know its *"CC"* for life. You guys helped shape my character. Even though, we were grown ass women *way* before our time, I am so proud of the productive women that we have become. Thanks for the love, memoirs and support. *Attorney* Lakesha Kintop, my best friend, my mentor, my muse, thanks girl. Corrine, Crystal, Vanessa *'Bamessa'*, and Juwania thanks for never judging me and being my friends 24-7 which, mostly required over time. Corrine, what would I do without you? My college crew, Lakesha Johnson, Latanya Beale, Candis Posey, & Candis Irving, thanks for allowing me to be me, to do me, you guys have branded my heart – you're the realest! Nyesha Maddix I haven't forgotten about you girl. You told me I was some kind of special and you could see me doing big things, girl those words alone inspired me to go hard! Thanks NaNa, I love you too. Sylvia Massey and Tracy Allen you two give the meaning to friends forever. Thanks for never leaving my life only allowing the time to change, and not letting time change you. Urmika Branch, "MI-MI", my partner in crime, girl you are my Thelma as I am your Louis, I love you girl. Yo-Yo and Laquesha thanks for keeping my hair buttered and thanks for that good old *Dime Piece* shoptalk. Quisha, thanks for all the 'real talks.' If nobody told it like it was, you made sure you did. Lashonda Stuwart, you know we go back to the burger bounce, back to the 80's baby! Mad love, Tiara (lil 1-2), Kamyia Laflore (you still my dawg) *Holla at cha girl.* O.M.W, you know who you are, thanks for loving me despite my flaws and faults, with no hidden agendas, you make me feel perfect, thanks for the unreserved love. To all my fallen soldiers that lost in this game of life, ya girl gon' try and play into over time just for you. To the only man that will ever have my entire heart, unconditionally, my daddy, Otis Moore Jr., *RIP*, I will forever be *Daddy's little Girl.* I'll never be whole without you. To John Carter "JC", my *appointed* big brother, I love and miss you. The streets are not the same without you. There's got to be *a heaven for a gangsta, RIP* big bro. To lil cuz Deon, Jeffery and Aunt Shelia, we will never forget your smiles, or your laugh – we miss you all. Life has changed without you. All my homies on lock down, no wall is strong enough to hold you forever, keep ya head up! Jeffery "Jigga" Coleman, one word-*TRU!* D.O.W.N... *Real recognize real and you look familiar. Thanks for being you...I miss you Jay.*

Donna Pettigrew-Jackson, thanks for translating my sloppy handwriting into a readable manuscript. You believed in Stiletto: 101, before it had a name. To Cans Bar & Canteen thanks for trusting me with your club and allowing me to bring in my b-day with a blast & a touch of class.

To the entire Milwaukee (Mil-talkie) it's our time to shine, lets blow up like the World Trade (no pun intended to the families who had loved ones lost on 9/11), let the world know, it's more to us than *Lavern and Shirley*, *That 70's show*, beer and cheese! They don't know it's going down in the *Mil-town* – do it look like we live on farms? They better recognize! ☺ To Reggie *"smooth as butta"* Brown, thanks for keeping me on blast and helping me represent. *Holla at cha girl...*

Last but not least, my publisher, KaShamba Williams of Precioustymes Entertainment, thanks for giving me the chance to prove myself to the world. You helped open the doors for me. Much love and respect to you. You are right – this is our year – PTE baby!! Joanie Smith, my editor, much respect and love to you. Thanks for sitting on the phone with me for hours – I do mean hours at a time – helping perfect what you say is... my baby. So, I owe the perfection of my first born to you. Call after 7pm, it's free!! ☺ Thanks gurl... holla!

Much love to all my family and friends, if I forgot anybody, please charge it to my mind and not my heart or better yet just charge it to the next book, I got you. ☺ Vendetta is coming at ya' neck soon!

To all the haters, you know who you are, this will probably be the only part of the book you remember, ☺ but you already know my motto: *GET ON MY LEVEL!!!* Thanks for helping promote and advertise me. I'm definitely feelin' that! Keep up the good work. The haters club has free admission. ENJOY!

To those that have purchased my book, THANK YOU for your support and always remember:

IN LIFE THERE ARE NO GUARANTEES, BUT IN GOD THERE ARE NO LIMITS.

It's YA GIRL,

LENAISE MEYEIL

Dedications

This book is dedicated to my father,
Otis Moore, Jr., and my *appointed* big brother,
John 'JC' Carter.

It hurts that you two can't be here to share this moment with me.

I would give it all up to have you back...

I love and miss you more than words can depict.

Foreword
By
KaShamba Williams

Stiletto 101: Don't Let The Stilettos Fool You is reflectively written for the fascinated high school graduate that wants to exchange hood drama for college drama! Modesty Blair is a young woman that was lead astray many times, but seemed to bandage her bruises and utilize her resources to become a college graduate. This novel exemplifies the hardship and trying times of being young and in love, while trying to make it to the top! It's uplifting to know that young men and women are beating the odds since; only 85 percent of African Americans graduate high school. And, out of that percentage, only 50 percent go forth to college. Nationwide, the college graduation rate for black students is an appallingly rate of 39 percent. However, it is a noted fact by The National Black United Fund that African Americans who enroll at a HBCU (Historically Black College University) is highly likely to graduate.

Modesty Blair testimony proves that attending an HBCU was the right decision for her. Her journey was short-lived, but worthy of being noted. Those late night parties, dates, and spring breaks didn't hold her back! She was at a distinct disadvantage being as though she was the first person in her family to commit to a four-year college, fresh out of high school. She strove hard to achieve and great possibilities were ahead for her. She overcame those barriers, just as other students can! So for those that are

10

struggling to make it - stick and stay! For those that have made it under extreme circumstances – HATS OFF TO YOU!

Enjoy the read!

~Remember, times are precious, never waste it on negativity~

Until next time,
Precioustymes

One Love, One Spirit,
KaShamba Williams

www.kashambawilliams.com

Check out the links to college resources:

http://scholarships.fatomei.com/african.html
http://students.washington.edu/bsu/scholarships.htm
http://www.sbac.edu/~nhs/Guidance/Minority.html
http://www.blackexcel.org/25scholarships.htm
http://www.mbna.com/about/foundation/index.html
http://hbcuconnect.com/scholarships.shtml
http://www.studentjobs.gov/d_scholarship.asp
http://www.sac100.com/Scholarships.htm
http://communityhigh.org/counseling/scholarship.html#schol
arships
http://www.collegeboundfoundation.org/aid/awards.cfm
http://www.fafsa.ed.gov/

Intro

I'm sitting at the college registrar's office, filling out my senior clearance form for graduation with a Colgate grin on my face. The single sheet of paper in front of me is the last fling with this college before walking across the stage, parading my famous Miss America wave to faculty members, students and attending guests. My last blessing to this college would be shaking hands with President of the School.

Who would have known that I would graduate from college exactly four years after high school? I had to pinch myself, because nine times out of ten, these days, if a person from the hood graduates from high school, that would be the accomplishment of a lifetime. Not me though, I was on my way in my stilettos to click-clack across the stage in front of everyone. Yeah, so Mr. Lynn, my high school counselor, can kiss my pretty ass. Instead of guiding and advising me in this direction, he gave me a farewell to welfare and jail – asshole!

I have to admit, I surprised my damn self, considering my background and my unplanned goals in life. My thoughts after high school consisted of: an easy pace job, a moneymaking hustler, a place of my own and just living it up ghetto fabulous. Little did I know, God had another path for me to follow! Unfortunately, I seemed to always find out His plans at the last minute.

Anyway, I am Modesty Yameyeia Blair and this is my testimony. I'm 22 years old, better known as *Motley*, a.k.a. to some as *'the bitch always wit' drama'*. Or, 'Ms. Motley'- as my grandmother (my father's mother) called me, because she said I was messy as a baby and the name sort of stuck with me. As special as I was to her, I didn't appreciate her while she was here on earth. I didn't take heed to her pearls of wisdom until she had passed on – rest her soul.

You've heard the saying, *'everybody has a story to tell.'* Well mine ain't to be told, but sold. So, here I am, dropping the real shit on this pad. It's best to hear it from the horse's mouth. 'Cause if you chose to hear it from the streets, the shit is guaranteed to be the fucked up version! You know how rumors get twisted and everybody adds at least one word before they pass it on.

My Aunt Lauren (my mother's) sister said I was cursed at birth, because in her mind, I was born to the worst combination of parents there could be. My mom was an undercover cokehead hustler and my dad was an abusive drug dealer. Aunt Lauren said if my mom and dad were ever to marry, they should change their last name to "Domestic Violence". (I thought that shit was funny as hell.) When I was younger, couldn't anybody tell me my grandma Ethel wasn't my momma. Most kids got upset when other people talked about their parents, but not me. I enjoyed all the stories about their hood rich life. We all lived in grandma's house: my mom, my dad, my older sister Maraca and me. Grandma performed all the parental duties; she was our rock and daddy footed the bills. Most times, drugs occupied my mom, Tracy Blair aka Tracy B.

My mom was 18 when she met my father and already nine months pregnant with Maraca. She was 19, when she got pregnant with me. Yes, that means (in case you're wondering) she had back-to-back pregnancies. My dad said the day he met my mother, she was walking down the street wobbling and crying 'cause she said some busta was following her. He offered her a ride home and from then on, for six years, she never left his side. What's funny is, my dad says when he thinks back to that day, my mom was probably never being chased; she just wanted to ride in his new candy apple red Corvette with plates reading, "Al's Toy". Everyone knew who Al was from being the neighborhood dope man. He was on the rise and his name was buzzing. Mom on the other hand was already pregnant by a low life and in need of an insurance policy (a.k.a. 'a sugar daddy')...and like ALLSTATE – she was in good hands with Al. My dad knew she was on some bullshit, but he didn't care. He wasn't that weak to her game. Although, it had slipped his mind once he saw mom's beautiful face...she was a mother pearl – gorgeous. I recall dad telling me he thought Tracy B was a fine Lil' mamma jamma; pretty as hell. She had long, straight, jet-black hair, light skin and was physically gifted. Let him tell it, her stomach wasn't that big, her ass was fat and he was trying to hit if she was willing to give it up. He bragged she was a bad bitch in her day. However, he also said if he knew she was a conniving little con artist, he would have left her sweet ass walking. I know he didn't mean it 'cause he loved to tell that story with the same enthusiasm every time; and every time I listened with the same bit of interest like I never heard him tell it before. My father's government name is Allen Smith, but to the people in the street you would think his nickname 'Alley Cat' was on his birth certificate. He was so fine he made Shemar Moore look like 2nd best.

It was routine for the administrators handling the birth certificates to question the parent(s) of the baby's name, but dad didn't think so. Tracy B had given me her last name 'cause my father refused to sign the birth certificate. They argued back and forth about it because dad said that's how niggas get their name in the system with all that child support bullshit. Eventually, dad had the last say and needless to say, that's why I have my mom's last name.

It was never a doubt I was daddy's prize possession even with him trippin' about putting his signature on my birth record. Lil' Motley was a daddy's girl. I was his first-born child that he cherished so much. The first gift he purchased for me was a small baby bracelet with 'Modesty' engraved across the back and 'Daddy's little girl' across the front. He had it made to adjust to my growing infant wrist. My first name was supposed to be Yameyeia, a name my mother got out of an African book, meaning 'Princess', but my father didn't agree with that so, they made it my middle name. He said everybody kept saying how pretty I was and how I always had a smirk on my face like a sincere thank you. He kept saying, *"My baby's so modest already, just like her daddy."* From that day I was born, he wanted Modesty to be my first name. My mother said to him, "That's some bullshit, because newborns don't smirk. How can you read that from an innocent baby's face?" She always suspected he got that name from one of his hos he was creeping with, but as long as he was taking care of home and she was getting hers, she didn't contest the name. Whatever daddy says... goes!

After six years of abuse and infidelity, Tracy B was sick of daddy's shit and decided to move to Milwaukee, leaving me behind with him and grandma Ethel. She wanted to start a 'new and improved' life with Maraca. She didn't actually leave me; she was just not allowed to take me. As a matter of fact, I don't think she even had enough courage to ask daddy if I could go. She didn't put up a fuss about leaving me behind; she just packed her bags and left like to hell wit' it. I'm not sure why Tracy B ran off, but every now and then, when grandma would get a little beer in her and daddy pissed her off, she never failed to remind him how he let a good woman get away over some crunked-up street bullshit. He chose the fast life over the only woman that truly had his back, but most do.

Surprisingly, Tracy B was doing her thing in Mil-town (Milwaukee). I had no idea our family

16

rolled so deep down this way; I had 'boo-coo' relatives. Living with daddy and grandma all those years kept me out of touch with my mother's side of the family. Don't get me wrong; I'm not saying the entire time I lived with daddy, I didn't speak to Tracy B and them. We kept in touch, but mostly through phone calls. I hadn't seen my aunts and cousins in years. Honestly, it had been so long that I probably wouldn't know who they were if they walked passed me. That was exactly why later, I was re-introduced to Aunt Lauren, her two girls, (Alize and Lasha), and Aunt Jessica, better known as 'Jessie', and her three daughters, (Taylor, Erica and Chanel). Now I could see where I got my feistiness. I came from a long line of thorough, strong headed, go-getting felines. Aunt Lauren was the brain of the family; she was good with numbers – a mathematician- so to speak. Aunt Jessica, I mean, Jessie, was the strong arm of the family. She emulated a man in every sense of the word, *literally*. She had a bald fade with waves that would shame any dude. It wasn't anything feminine about her except the woman she kept on her arm. I never got a chance to get acquainted with Aunt Jessie that well outside of the fact that she was the black sheep of the family, caught a dope case, and was now facing 15 for that shit. Shalonda, her live-in lover cared for her kids while she was away. Talk about a dysfunctional family - they were far from '*My wife and Kids*' with Damon Wayans and Tisha Campbell. But, enough of the family history, 'cause that shit digs deep and if I keep talking about them, I wouldn't have enough time to tell you how I got where I am today, or tell you some of the stories that go along with my journey. Walk with me...

Chapter One

I can remember back to when I applied to Lane College (LC), in Jackson, Tennessee. I only did it to hush up my best friend, Jurnee. She had gotten on my last nerves sweatin' me to apply for college. When I finally told her I was in route, she was thrilled since she had enrolled at the college the year before. We became best friends when I transferred to the same high school she attended in Milwaukee from Chicago. This was a major move for me after grandma Ethel died of a heart attack. I think she passed from a broken heart rather than a heart attack, because shortly after daddy was indicted on drug conspiracy and got 10 years federal time – no parole, no time cuts for good behavior, nothing, but 10 long years, her heart stopped pumping. After the arrangements, I was forced to move with Tracy B, Maraca and Austin.

My daddy's sister, Aunt Kelly still resided in Chicago, but was a full time Airline career woman. While she was close with my dad, she still harbored ill feelings about my mother for how she up and left me. I wanted to stay in Chicago with her, but she was full of excuses. She was like, "I love you baby, but things are too busy down at the in-flight office. I do too much traveling to be trying to raise somebody else's child. Your mother is the one who cocked her legs open to Al, so it's time for her to step up and play the 'momma' role." So, nine years later, after Tracy B had sprung, I was mauled to Milwaukee to start a new life with my maternal mother.

Once I situated in my new school, my life seemed to carry on like it had never changed. I quickly adjusted to my surroundings. That's where I met Jurnee. We didn't really click off top. She hung with the popular girls that everybody admired and wanted to be like. I hung with the not so popular girls that people knew, but rarely admired. But, I stood out amongst them all. I was pretty, petite and dressed nice; that's how I got Jurnee's attention. She seemed to like profiling herself with girls *almost* as pretty as her that could dress *almost,* as nice as she did. I say almost, 'cause to her, she was always on top; and her crew a notch under her, but never over her.

Jurnee would frequently strike up small conversations with me in homeroom, or during lunch, complimenting me on my gear. It was enough to let me know she viewed me on her clique's status. She knew how to play it, not complimenting me too much, because, of course, she didn't want me to think I could fuck wit' her. Admittingly, Jurnee Luna was a very pretty girl though. She wasn't fairly short or tall, she was in between the two, with a golden brown complexion; like she was mixed with Philippine or something. She might have been. She wouldn't know 'cause her father looked the same way, but he didn't know his family. He was lost in the world of adoption as a child. Jurnee had good hair too. She's what the dudes down south called, "*stout junk*." All the boys at our high school liked her, but most of the guys were wimps and afraid to approach her. Her presence was intimidating too most - both females and males. She was only 15, but by looks and the way she acted - she thought she was a grown-ass woman. Brandon, this boy I barely knew, warned me she was dumb as a blonde and bad news as a friend. Later I found out he was a rejectee, so that explains the hating.

Seeing as how I had always been a 'shoe princess,' my first conversation with Jurnee was about my kicks. She looked me up and down, digging my shoes.

"I like those, where you get 'em?" Oh, she was really envious of them.

Of course, to everything she asked, I'd say, "Chi", (that's short for Chicago.) I knew that impressed her too. I learned that black folk in Mil-town loved that Chi-town flava. Shit, most of them even claimed to be from there. Jurnee hung with Micole, Linda, and Tammy. Micole was a hot-ass 14 year old caught up in teen pregnancy. This girl couldn't stand me. But I didn't give a rat's ass because I knew she was hatin' that 'I was the new girl taking attention from her. I heard she used to say I was ugly and too skinny. At the time, her and Jurnee were best friends but I rarely saw this broad for her to be talkin' that 'rah-rah' shit. We spoke cordially when we grouped together on some, '*I wish she would say something out of the way to me'* frontin' like a mothafucka. Tammy was a senior and only attending half days at school because she had enough credits to do so without attending full-time to graduate, which eventually caused her to branch off to do her own thing. Then, there was Linda. She was an inch taller than me, had a bob hair cut brown with blonde streaks flowing through. Her skin was bronze in complexion that had a cute little mole right under her left eye. This girl was definitely video type cast and had the dance skills to top that off. I knew she couldn't wait to get close to me 'cause when she did - she was quick to ask to borrow my clothes. We happened to be in the same art class together, but we didn't sit together. She was always drilling me about Chicago. Initially, I don't think she believed I was from there. After I answered her '21 questions' bullshit - the run down from hood to hood -the skating rink to the mall - she must have been convinced, 'cause she stopped asking after a while. Either that, or Linda didn't know what the hell I was talking about. So, she shut up when I mentioned places she didn't recognize. She would point out things like - the Lark, Michigan Street or Bryers, but anybody with a taste for fashion and had loot went to those popular stores in Chi to shop. Eventually, Linda invited me to sit with them at lunch after art class. By this time, Micole had left school to have her baby, so I was now the replacement of the crew. I fit right in like a link hadn't been missing. Micole probably envied that shit. Linda and I were the coolest at first; I even started to sit with her in art class, gaining her trust quickly. I could tell 'cause she was always telling me her dark secrets. Once, she had sex with this guy named Tyson (that was supposed to be her man), gave her a STD (sexually transmitted disease). She was scared to tell him and she wanted my advice. I was still a virgin, so I'm like, "Shiiit, I'd go off... curse his ass out. That's nasty—fuck that."

She was like, "Even if he was your man and you loved him?"

So I reply, "The fool must don't love you cause he gave you a disease. Why y'all didn't use a rubber? It's too many diseases out there not to be using protection!"

She got real quiet, stood back, looked at me with a screwed up face, popping her chewing gum. She frowned, "Hell naw...I don't believe this shit...you *must* be a virgin. Here I am telling you my bid'ness, and you haven't even had that thang tapped yet. How you gon' give me advice?"

"What does that have to do with anything?" I whipped back.

"Common sense...'cause any bitch know if you the wifey, you don't demand no dumb shit like that. Yo' man ain't gonna use no condom, and if you ask him to wear one, he'll think you fuckin' off."

"Shit, you must not be the wifey because if you were, he'd consider wearing a jimmy with the other broad he creepin' with. Don't get it confused. You need to check him...giving diseases away like gifts," I screamed on her.

Rolling her neck and sucking her teeth, she called herself busting it down to me, "All niggas got other hos. Anyway, I'm not asking for your input. I'm just asking you how I should tell him." She smacked her lips and looked at me with disappointment when I didn't immediately respond, "Fuck it then. I thought you would understand."

I felt sorry for her because her spot was blown up and she felt embarrassed by telling me. She didn't look in my face for the rest of the class. So after class, I told her I would help her. My scheme was to call him, fake like a girl named Keisha, (all niggas knew a Keisha and most are triflin' as hell) curse him out like he gave it to me and hang up before he questioned it. Once he found out, he'd be worried and would either tell on himself, go get checked out, or ignore it. Poor Linda, she should have just plain out told him. She was a bag of nerves and afraid he might think she gave it to him. I heard some guys were good in turning the tables on you, like you were the one fucking around. They use that reverse psychology bullshit. Anyway, it must have made her feel better, because she liked the idea. She hugged me and said, "Thanks, it's a plan. We'll run it tonight on the three-way." I still had my own thoughts and comments in my head, but decided to keep it to myself. It wasn't worth another stressful convo with Linda about her 'so-called' man.

I sat with the clique everyday at lunch and talked to Linda on the phone almost every night. We, in due time, became full-time partners in crime.

Chapter Two

Basketball season was approaching and everywhere you turned flyers were posted for try-outs. I played at my old school back in Chicago so I figured I'd tryout. It also kept me physically fit. I wasn't trying to develop a cottage cheese ass for sitting around not wanting to participate in shit. I was trying to keep my figure tight. I was a'ight, no major ball skills, but I knew the game and I was fast. Surprisingly, Jurnee played too. She was already one of the return players from last season. She was on varsity, first string and could ball her ass off. I never would have known "Ms. Grown-Ass," got involved in extra curricular activities. She didn't have to tryout, but her and all the other returning players still did all of the exercises during try-outs. Linda even came to the gym to chance her luck. She only lasted two days of tryouts before she started to complain. She was like, "Hell naw, my body is too sore for this shit. I can't take it." Obviously, the b-ball game wasn't as strong as Tyson's, because she stopped coming to practice all together; she preferred playing ball on his courts and his work-outs better. The coach was an older black man with salt and pepper hair, Coach Hayman. He was cool and real serious about his team. I made JV, starting point guard, #25 (not bad for a transferring sophomore student coming on to an already established team). I wasn't even mad

about not making varsity, 'cause at my other
school I didn't even start on the freshman team.
Coach was impressed by my swiftness and I was
pretty good performing all the basics. My jump
shots were broke, but could be improved. I
dribbled well, no fancy stuff but I was hella quick
on fast breaks.

Jurnee and I practiced together everyday,
pairing up on partner exercises. One day after
practice her boyfriend didn't show to pick her up,
so Ms. Thing had to swallow her pride and walk
to the bus stop with me. She was pissed: whining
like she wanted to cry.

"Ugh! This nigga get on my nerves. He's
probably somewhere in some hood rat's face. I
don't know why I even deal with Kevin's ass."

She had a big herringbone around her neck
that he bought for her. Confiding in me that he
didn't have a job and how, he *used* to go to our
school. I figured he must sell dope like most did,
and yep, I was right. Less than 10 minutes after
we got to the bus stop, a burgundy Chevy pulled
up with shiny gold 18 inch rims and tinted
windows, thumpin' from the music. When the
driver side window came down, a rolling cloud of
smoke escaped like thick steam.

She immediately went off on him. "I told
you to pick me up at 6 o'clock."

He smiled and said, "Girl, get yo' ass in this
car," and eased the window back up. I caught a
quick glimpse of him. Kevin was light skinned

with long wavy hair like Snoop Dog when he wore his shit out; all the playa-playas wore their hair in this style. Her lips were tight as she tried to play it off.

"Modesty, I'm sorry I gotta go. I would ask him to drop you off, but the nigga is so ignorant, I know he won't. I'll get your number from Linda and call you tonight, okay?" Like a trained pup, she jumped into the car and they pulled off before I could even answer. It was cool though. I was wondering when we would start to kick it outside of basketball practice and the lunchroom. I had to catch the bus home by myself. I only lived up the street anyway, not walking distance, but not a long bus ride either. Kids 10 and under paid $1.25 in bus fare. That's what I dropped in the fare collector and righteously walked to my seat. I wasn't that small, but I knew the bus driver wouldn't challenge me. Eventually, coach gave us bus passes and I didn't have to cheat the bus company anymore.

We lived in a small two-bedroom apartment. Tracy B had her private quarters on one side of the apartment while Maraca, Austin (my bad-ass little brother that Tracy B snuck in there) and I squeezed in one room. It was tight, but we made out o.k. I shared a bunk bed, (twin size at the top and full size mattress at the bottom) with my sister. Austin had a small twin size bed on the opposite side of us. I had no choice but to get to know them better with us living in that little ass room.

Maraca went to a different high school than I did. So far, we got along fine – no major problems. She was never home, always shacked up with a new buck named Tojoe, who moved around the way. Maraca staked her claim on him and was damn near living with him without Tracy B's consent. Austin slept on the couch most of the time watching TV until he fell asleep. So, I pretty much had the room to myself. He was a pest and bad as fuck. Tracy B, used to beat the hell out that boy. He was suspended from school every other month for different violations, and no matter how much he cried and pleaded when he got whooped, he'd get suspended again. It was his routine. I didn't understand the boy. He would hide under the bed and eavesdrop, listening to me on the phone. He especially showed out when my friends came over. He was a pain in my derriere. His father's name was, Nelson Anderson; he never came around. Ain't no telling where he was – he called every now and then. Tracy B says Austin looked a lot like him, so I could picture what his daddy might look like if he never came around. My little brother was short, skinny, dark with low wavy hair, big shiny dark eyes and a small pea head. He's cute, but he acted like a girl sometimes. I prayed he didn't grow up to be a homo. He did live in a house with three women, so the possibility could exist.

Tracy B, let us do pretty much what we wanted to do - just the girls at this point. Rather, she never questioned our whereabouts, as long as we came home safe. Even with her 'behind the door' bad habits, she kept us dipped in the newest fads. We got a pair of shoes every time a fly pair came out. Despite what I thought about her in the past, she was a cool mother. She didn't seem to use drugs anymore or I just couldn't tell. I think getting high was a scapegoat from daddy's beatings anyway. She did seem to take up a new hobby though... getting young dick. She had a different man in her room every Friday. We never talked about it either. It often bothered me to see all those different young men coming up in our crib to see her. I used to cry secretly, *"my momma is a ho'."*

As far as boys went, she never asked me if I was having sex or not. I could tell she thought I was from they way she watched me, but I never brought it up. Truth is, I don't think she really cared, as along as I didn't bring home no packages (a sexual disease or a pouched stomach).

Chapter Three

Grandma Ethel had gon' home almost a year and I hadn't even heard from daddy. He had to know I knew he was in jail. He couldn't send a kite (letter) home? It's fucked up when a man can have kids on the outside of the joint and have nothing but time to write them and don't. Then one day...out of nowhere - he called. I was mad, but happy to hear from him on my sweet 16th birthday. Instead of a warm reception, he started throwing questions, interrogating me like the damn police, wanting to know about Tracy B.

"Modesty how is your mother? Is she still fine? Does she still love a nigga? Do she have a man? Where y'all living? Is the place nice? Are they treating you right? How's your sister? You still keeping your hair tight? Is it still long? Is it longer than your mother's? Do you miss me? Are you mad at me? Are you still daddy's little girl?" He finally came up for air. Then, he hit me with... "Are you out there telling my damn business?"

I had to slow him down like, "Dag, daddy! What is it? Slow down!"

I knew it had been a year, but dang he acted like he would never talk to me again. However, I answered most of the questions. I lied about my hair though. Me, Tracy B and Maraca all went and got our hair cut together. I had my honey blonde hair cut short at the top with little curls on the side, with it still hanging long in the back. I didn't tell daddy though, he would have snapped. It was something about him and long hair. Maraca's hair was dark red like Tracy B's.

After all that fuss, Daddy told me he was doing well and he was locked up with most of the guys he ran with on the streets. So, he was straight. I wasn't too concerned about that because I knew my dad could hold his. But he did say something that made my ears twitch – since he was locked up, Tracy B was given power of attorney over his portion of my grandma's estate, which, I didn't know.

"You know your grandma Ethel loved you right?"

"Yes daddy, I know that."

"She loved you so much that she left you the balance of her estate... $60,000, but you can't touch it until you turn the magic age of 18."

I felt like screamin', "*Awww shit! Seize the day... Got-damn!*" The timing was great, 'cause I was in Driver's Education this semester. So, seeing that I was the main source of Tracy B's cash flow, I decided to ask for a car and a Dooney and Burke purse for my birthday.

"Daddy you know I'm in Driver's Ed this semester and I'm passing the class with flying colors. I'm good at it; when I test drove, the teacher even commended me on my skills."

"That's my girl, that's how we do – we ace our shit! When will you get your official driver's license?"

"My final exam is a month away. I know I'ma pass it!" I anticipated that he was leading up to what I was going to ask... for a car!

"If you pass that test, and I know you will, have Tracy B take you out to buy you a car for no more than $1200."

"Thank you Daddy!" I screamed for my mom to hear, "I knew you would come through on the car tip." All the kids my age had hoop-dies anyway. With that amount, I would find a car with $1,000 and use $200 to get me a CD player put in it. Tracy B overheard my end of the conversation, rolled her eyes and snatched the phone out of my hand.

"Al that damn girl don't need a car at 16 years old. You keep spoiling her! I got other mouths to feed. Have you considered that?"

I could only imagine what daddy was saying to her, but I knew whatever it was, it shut her up. When she got off the phone, her whole attitude had changed from the look on her disturbed face. I thought it was 'cause she had to buy me a car, but to my surprise, I found out that daddy had just dropped a bomb on her: he was getting married, in jail, to his new woman that he met through B.P. Love's jailhouse connection newsletter. Ain't that a bitch?

"Ya' daddy is about to do some dumb shit! He's getting married while in jail to a woman he really don't know. That's the worse move a man in jail can make."

I frowned at her and with mixed emotions and asked, "Why didn't he tell me? And, why did he hang up without speaking back to me?"

She just stood there paralyzed, looking at me with blank stare. "He said he loves you and he'll call back next week." She just couldn't shake the thought of daddy getting married; a few seconds after that, she broke down and cried like a baby as if they were still together. I guess first loves are hard to shake even if the relationship was abusive. In tears, she confessed, they kept in touch after she moved away and she still loved him deep down. Grandma Ethel coaxed him to still take care of her and Maraca as his own when they left. He did, but when she got pregnant with Austin. He told her to let the new nigga inherit the responsibilities. It was apparent that she was devastated by the future marriage. I knew 'cause she locked herself in her room for the rest of the night. That was the last time we heard from daddy. We wrote to him occasionally, but he never wrote back after getting married. I was upset with him, but I kept the letters flowing just to keep him updated on every aspect of my life, even though he didn't respond. I assumed he got the picture that I was no longer 'daddy's little girl' from some of the shit I wrote him.

♥ ♥ ♥ ♥ ♥

For my birthday, Maraca got me a fake ID so we could club hop. Even though she wasn't of age – only 17 – she had a fake ID also. Exactly one month after my birthday as a late celebration me, Maraca and the crew went to a 21 and up club called, *'The Red Corvette'*. It was going down... we were ready to get our swagger on. I wore some black fitted pants with a tan Guess dress shirt that matched my new tan Dooney and Burke purse. It went perfect with my black stiletto boots from Nine West. We were young, but we were flossin' like the older chicks. We packed five deep, in my new to me, but used, Buick Century car. Yeah, daddy did come through! We rolled up to the club, trying to out sing each other bumping Tupac's memorable song, *Me and My Girlfriend,* feeling like the song was about each of us not even knowing he was giving praise to his gun. As we neared the door, I became very nervous and didn't want to get 'bust out' by security. However, we got in smoothly, no questions asked. A cute face and a fat ass most times will get you in... you just have to know how to work ya' shit. Once inside, I was kickin' it with the party people. Most of our classmates were there with fake ID's, just like us. I wasn't the least surprised to see that Maraca knew everybody. She kept introducing me to a lot of people. Telling them, "This is my little sister y'all, Modesty. Today is her birthday." She was lying, but was getting niggas to purchase drinks doing so. I was happy nobody asked how old I was. If they'd asked, I would have lied and boosted my age up. A dude named Michael looked me over like he had x-ray vision to see through my shit. Then he blurted out, "Dayumn! Maraca, I didn't know you had a little sister this fine. Y'all real sisters?" He examined both of us over trying to find any similarities. I thought he asked 'cause of the difference in our skin complexion. I was high yellow like my dad's side of the family and Maraca was the ebony version of Tracy B. Michael had Maraca vexed; she flipped out on his ass. "Yeah, nigga. She's my blood and off limits to you...so just step!" Then turning to me she said, "Modesty, stay the fuck away from him. He's a male prostitute, pussy don't have no face to him... with his broke-ass!" When we all clowned on his ass, he walked away. Maraca's boyfriend Tojoe captivated her attention after that, so I didn't see her again until we loaded back in the car. The boy Michael tried to get at me again and I didn't know if Maraca was serious or not about what she said about him, so I stayed away. I pulled my girl Linda on the dance floor and we bugged off of every song like we was at a high school dance.

The older broads turned their noses up at us. They were just jealous 'cause we could break it down, especially off of Trina's, *'I'm The Baddest Bitch'.* The freak came out of Linda when she heard that. She got buck wild, hollering, *"This my shit!"* Some short sweaty guy got on her from the back, grinding her ass. That's when I exited and went to the bar to sit next to Jurnee and my second cousin, Tyler. His ugly gorilla-face friend was eyeing me. I didn't want him to think nothing was jumping off so I gave him the look like, *'don't even think about it nigga,'* then turned the other way and ordered a Pepsi, since I wasn't big on drinking – I hadn't gotten use to the taste of liquor at this point. Tracy B had let me taste a sip of whiskey once before and that shit was horrible – that shit turned me off to liquor but not for too long. I spotted this fine-ass chocolate dream on the other side of the bar. He had me uttering, *Damn!!! Who is that?* He was hella fine tall, dark and baldheaded. He reminded me of Michael Jordan. Naw, not that fine, but he was damn close! Yeah, Mike still gets his props from me. Shit, he ain't with Juanita anymore... is he? MJ holla at ya' girl – I'm single! Jurnee blurted out, "Oh, that's JJ. He plays basketball for Washington High School." I didn't give a fuck who he played for; I wanted him on my team! If he was taken (and honestly it wouldn't have mattered), I was stepping on some chickenhead's toes if he was.

"Whose man is he?" I nosed, playing him close with my eyes.

"Girl, I don't know. I know of him from around, but not like that. He is fine, isn't he?"

"Hell yeah, you ain't never lied 'bout that!" I was already on my way to find Linda so she could hook me up. We always did that for each other. Linda's wild ass was in the middle of the dance floor dancing on her knees in a crowd off her tenth song since I'd left her on the dance floor. I'm glad I caught her that hussy had to cool down anyway. I pulled her up off the floor and yelled over the loud music.

"Bitch, this ain't no damn basement party; you acting all hoochie."

She was feeling her liquor; so she just laughed and waved it off. We were close enough I could talk to her like that. I pointed at JJ and said, "Hook me up." She already knew the business and went at him. I watched as Linda pulled the tail of his shirt.

"Your name JJ right?"
"Who wanna know?" he replied to her.
"You see my girl over there," she pointed at me and I twiddled my three fingers to say hello to him.

"Baby girl looking real slick, but you can tell her if she wanna talk to me, come rap to me herself."

"Alright, playa!" Linda turned away cheesin' (smiling) toward the ladies room.

When Linda walked in a different direction, I thought he dissed me. That's what we did when niggas weren't interested or said their girl was around - we walked in another direction. That was our language – we knew that meant – no match! I blew air from my mouth and began to walk away thinking, too damn bad! To my surprise, that's when he signaled for me to come over. I loved that bitch (Linda), figuratively speaking - but she played too much. She hadn't changed the script; her drunk-ass had to piss. Anyway, I got over to JJ, holding in my smile, trying' to be cool.

He introduced himself, "Hey, pretty. Wuz' up? I'm JJ."

"I'm Modesty."

"Modesty, huh? Pretty name, ma... you look a little young though." He was trying to feel me out. I got a little nervous, so I decided to lie. I figured he had to be at least 18, too young to be in the club, so why was he stuntin' on me?

"Good black don't crack, I'm 21. Today's my birthday."

"Happy Birthday," he replied. "Do you want a drink?"

I declined, "No thank you, I don't drink."

JJ eyes raced around my body. "Do you dance?" He licked his lips like he was ready to get VIP treatment.

"What... *strip*?"

"Naw, do you wanna go on the dance floor?"

I almost played myself; both of us laughed at my lewdness and headed for the dance floor. We slow danced off of R. Kelly's, *Bump & Grind* track. His warm breath mumbled the words in my ear, making my coochie lips moist. He smelled so damn good. I don't know what type of cologne he had on, but if I were to name it, it would be called, "Get the pussy on GP!" This nigga was holdin' me tight, massaging my back while we grooved. In his case, milk did a body **damn** good! Then... oops, while I was enjoying the feel of his massive chest and his arm muscles, his dick got jealous and decided to rise to the occasion too. His '*Richard*' felt huge. It was rock hard from me rolling and pumping my fat ass on him. I was still a virgin, but the way I worked my moves, you would never know it. We exchanged digits after the club. I got his pager number and I gave him my house number. This nigga had me gassed. That slow grind had us both going. It wouldn't be long before I would lose my virginity to him... that was a given! When we got home, somehow Tracy B found out we were in the 21 and up and she went the fuck off!

"What the hell wrong with you, Modesty! You got a car and think you're grown!" She couldn't wait to throw that shit up. "I don't care who you were with! I better not hear about your grown ass in a club no more! You're getting beside yourself. Now I advise you to slow it up, girl. And Maraca, why did you take her? She asked as if she was of age to get in with a real ID. "It's bad enough your ass is wild and out of control! I don't need two fast ass hos living wit' me. I'm putting a stop to this dumb shit right now!!"

Maraca was a few months pregnant by Tojoe (and mom knew about it), but she wasn't no ho' like Tracy B claimed her to be. We stuck together and looked at our mother like she'd lost her mind. It was no need for her to try and play the Momma role now, when she didn't hum a word about anything else. Speaking of a 'ho'... some high yellow, young nigga with long hair that we seen earlier at the club came bopping out of her room into the bathroom; and his arrogant-ass had nerve to interrupt and speak to us in the middle of family business. I know he was every bit of Maraca's age. I couldn't quite put my finger on it, but he looked familiar as hell not just from the club either. He even had his tinted out burgundy Chevy on them gold rims, parked in our driveway. How was Tracy B gon' chastise somebody when she fucking somebody's teenage son?

We thought we were grown enough to handle ours, so hell yeah...we went out every weekend after that. Maraca didn't even stress over her pregnancy; she partied like, *"What the fuck? Can I live?"*

Chapter Four

It was junior year – Jurnee, Linda and I were hanging tight. Occasionally, I still hung with my other friends, the 'not so popular girls,' Iesha, Charo and Marie. They didn't seem to mind my transition from the new girl to one of the most popular girls. Actually, they seemed to admire it. Whenever I would hang with them, they'd be on some 'groupie' type shit, asking questions like, *"How does Jurnee act? Is she cool or stuck up?"* They didn't believe me when I told them, yeah; she was cool and how much fun we had together. They were shocked when I told them we go out to 21 and up clubs. They wouldn't dare step foot in a club! These were some real boxed cut schoolgirls. Jurnee thought they were slow, but really, we were just fast hot tail girls, playing grown ups and they were the ones that would be on the corporate come up, hiring us. Of course we had those who hated on us or on Jurnee rather, 'cause I was cool with everybody sociably – she wasn't. She didn't hang with anybody outside of Linda and me at school. At this point, she only spoke to people if they spoke first. Eventually that led to unnecessary enemies. Girls would be like *"fuck her"* (talking about Jurnee). *"I'll whoop her ass." "I'll cut the bitches hair!" "She ain't shit with her big funky ass." "I'll have my people jump her."* They were jealous of her and just hating 'cause she didn't fuck with

them like that.   Although, she could be anti-
social most times – I didn't realize it had gotten
that serious. We knew that it would cause trouble
sooner or later, but who would've thought it
would be with one of our basketball teammates?
The girl's name was Kenyatta, but they called her
Kenny. Jurnee said they probably called her
Kenny 'cause she looked like a boy. Most thought
she was a dyke because she was built husky,
walked hard and kept her hair cut low like a
dude.   She hung with Tonya and Kim who were
ghetto as hell, thugged out broads... straight from
the hood. I was too, but at least you couldn't tell
until I got mad. They were straight hood rats and
wore that title proudly.   Kenny's reason for
starting the fight was because she accused
Jurnee of looking at her crazy all the time and
fouling her on purpose in practice. Which was a
lie, 'cause Kenny was always walking 'round
starting fights for no reason. Jurnee knew it was
coming. She just didn't know when, but damn...
did it have to happen on picture day? We were all
dressed up to take pictures for the yearbook,
looking fly... and those dumb bitches started right
after lunch before we could get our pictures
taken.   We were walking up the stairs, Jurnee,
Linda, and I. Kenny yelled out, "Fuck her... fake
ass, Pocahontas."   We knew she was talking
about Jurnee, since she was the only one whose
hair hung down her back. I had my hair cut chin
length and tapered in the back.   Linda had
shoulder length hair, pulled back in a ponytail.

Jurnee smacked her lips, "Here we go, Modesty. Are you going to help me if that big bitch try and fight me?" She was scared, but ready to deal with the drama. I was ready to ride with her thinking all they really wanted was to see if the pretty girls could get down for theirs.

"You think Linda will help?" she whispered to me.

"She better or we gonna whoop her ass after we finish these hos." I was fueling. We didn't even have to ask Linda 'cause she had already taken off her big *'Around the Way Girls'* hoop earrings. Jurnee was pissed and all she kept saying, "I know these hood rats are going straight for my hair! Chicken head ho's..." She yelled out like a raging roar from a lion, "BITCHES MAD 'CAUSE MY SHIT DIPPIN' THAT ALL!" She was right; these baldhead bitches were going directly for the tresses. That's the way they fought... dirty and real dirty at that. We were walking towards Linda's locker, so she could get her pad lock. I knew she was from "Chi" then 'cause that's how my girls and I threw down back in the day. Bust-a-bitch with a padlock, I bet they don't mess with you after that! That made me reminisce, not for long though. Kenny was right behind us with her 'he-she' posse in tow. She bumped Jurnee hard and said, "Excuse you, you big head ho'." Before I knew it, Jurnee charged Kenny. I didn't even look back; I dove right in arms swinging. We were tearing her ass up – Linda did her part by jumping on Kim. Tonya (Kenny's girl) snatched me off of Kenny. That's when we started fighting

44

head up. I'm not gonna lie, Tonya was warming my ass up. She had me pinned on the ground. I couldn't even see Linda or Jurnee fighting anymore. I just heard people like, "*Oooh! A fight! A fight!*" I got a couple of good licks in, but Tonya had overpowered me. This boy Chris, the class clown, was shouting, "*Damn! Modesty getting her ass stomped.*" I heard that shit and it boosted me to get wilder. I was still losing the battle trying to tag her ass too. This bitch was out of control! Not to make any excuses or anything, but she was bigger than me... and heavy set, a Sasquatch looking bitch. Thinking back to that day, Tonya, you got that! Security broke it all up after awhile; we made a big ass scene. They took us to different empty rooms. My face felt like fire. That's how bad it felt and it was stinging and throbbing. I touched it to see if I was bleeding. It wasn't, but I felt a large welt stretching from my nose to my ear. I prayed I didn't have a black eye or any knots. Shit, I was wondering who won the other two fights. Jurnee or Kenny? ...Linda or Kim? One of them had to represent since I took an 'L' (loss) on that one. I was content with that because all fighters lose at least once in their careers. This so-happened to be mines. I reached for my purse to get my cell phone to call Maraca to come up here and meet me after school. When I noticed it was gone, I shouted, "Hell naw! Let me out this mothafucka! My purse is gone!" I don't know what the hell I was thinking, like I could hold onto a purse and fight. That's what I get with that 'pretty girl' shit. Security asked me to,

"Calm down," as he sat guarding the door like I was in protective custody. Good thing Otis was one of the cool ones though another security guard may have put the pressure on me. He used to let us skip class and walk the halls with him, like he was escorting us somewhere. This was the same man we would see at the club. He was cute and looked about 23 years old. I knew he was off limits; the principal would have his job if he dipped off with any of the students. Otis laughed when he saw how short tempered I was. He said, "Shorty, what you doing fighting? I thought you and ya' girls were ladies and above all this childish stuff?" Before I snapped back at that, I asked him, "Do I have a black eye." "No, it's just a little red," he teased. "The scratches on your face are swollen, but they'll fade away." Still examining me from head to toe he stated, "Your little yellow ass got bruises on your arm and on your neck." I blushed 'cause that was a hicky JJ gave me the night before. I asked him, "Did anybody pick up my purse? And, where are my girls?" He replied, "Jurnee is in the principal's office with Coach Hayman and Kenny, explaining what this fight was about and Linda is in a room directly across from you."

"Otis, I need to find my purse. Can you help me?" Desperate times, call for desperate measures, I needed my shit back. I described my purse to him and asked if he could go check on that for me. This was my black leather Coach purse with a pocket on the front and a long adjustable strap we were talking about. Soon as he walked away, I ran over to Linda's room. She was over there with the school nurse crying. I didn't know what to think. When I walked in, the nurse walked out and Linda hugged me.

"You a'ight? Damn, you lost that bad they called medical help and shit?" I was joking; she didn't even look like she was in a rumble like I had. Her ponytail was a little cocked to the side, that's all. We both laughed, glad about the release of tension (for the moment).

"Girl, pul-leaze! Kim's monkey-ass can't fight. She didn't even know what to do when she ran up on me. She tried to strong arm me but I went 'buck the fuck' wild on that ho."

"Damn, I should have been fighting her, 'cause Tonya opened up a family sized can of whoop ass on me.... ole' girl put the size 9 Timbs on my ass." At that thought, we broke out laughing again. "So, why are you crying then? You got the bitch, I didn't. I'm the one that should be crying."

"Gurl, I'm pregnant and that bitch could have made me have a miscarriage."

"Pregnant? Whoa...back up! Where did this come from? Bitch, why you ain't tell me?"

"Duh, stupid! I just did."

"What you mean, you just did?"

"I mean... before I wasn't sure until last night. I was gonna tell y'all when we went to the shop to get our nails and toes done."

"Who you pregnant by? ... Tyson?"

She put her hands on her hips, looking at me like I was always asking stupid questions. "Of course," she frowned. Our conversation was interrupted when Otis walked in with my purse in his hand. I went through it immediately; only to find that my cell phone was gone, my pager, and my damn fifty dollars that I had for my nails and gas. I was really pissed then. Before I could call home, my momma, Maraca and two cousins, Taylor and Erica, were already at the front desk asking where I was. Taylor and Erica were ready for round two. I was wondering how they knew so quickly, they went to high school across town with Maraca. Loud and ready, "WHERE 'DEM HOS AT?" they asked in unison. I laughed 'cause they made it seem like I called them up there.

"Well, Motley... did you win or lose? 'Cause you know you think you bad... all that shit you be talking." Maraca was trying to hype me up.

"Hell yeah, I won... what you think?" I lied. Why tell them the truth and risk my rep with my big sister? My mother looked at us and rolled her eyes. She was too busy flirting, putting the moves on Otis, the security guard. Jurnee's grandmother and her father came for her. Sad, but nobody showed for Linda that was fucked up, so my mother claimed her as her niece. We were all suspended for 3 days and each given a $150 ticket for disorderly conduct by the Milwaukee

County police. When we went to court it was dropped 'cause Kenny and her crew were already known as troublemakers. Kenny was allowed back to school based upon her involvement with the basketball team, but Kim and Tonya got kicked out, so they went to another school. Too bad for them ho's! Tonya better know, karma comes back quicker to the giver... watch ya' back bitch!

Chapter Five

The high school year was almost over. Track season had started and my name was buzzing. Last track season, I won the city indoor meet for the fastest female in the 55-meter dash and the 220-yard dash. Jurnee was graduating a year early because she had enough credit hours; and Linda barely came to school anymore. We talked a few times of week. She was living with her baby daddy, Tyson, playing house. Jurnee and I were best friends by the time she graduated. We were so close; we told each other everything and had become inseparable. For graduation, her sister and I got together and threw Jurnee a "graduation, going-away-to-college" barbeque. Jurnee had gotten accepted to three schools. One in Milwaukee, Marquette University; one in Whitewater, University of Wisconsin-Whitewater, (that's about a half hour away) and lastly, Lane College in Jackson, Tennessee. She chose Lane College (LC) because she had a full academic scholarship and thought it would be better to get further away. Her mother's side of the family was originally from Jackson and Humboldt, Tennessee, so she had distant relatives down there. She was leaving, moving to the dirty south for some southern education. I was sad she was going (and secretly angry with her for leaving me.) She could have graduated with my class, but she bounced a year early. Before she flew the coup, we went and got tattoos. She got a big tinker bell dragonfly on her arm and I got a butterfly on my back with Modesty written under it. That was the most painful situation I could have put myself in. They are additive though 'cause I got three more after that not even worrying about the risks that came with getting them.

The barbeque turned out better than we thought it would. We had 36th Street jumpin'. We barbequed in Tally's (Jurnee's cousin) backyard and it was crackin'. It was a hood family affair. Everybody and anybody were there. We made flyers and went to most of the high schools and passed them out. People we didn't know came. That was cool 'cause we were kickin' it. Somehow everybody there was linked in some kind of way. That's just how Milwaukee was - everybody knew everybody. Even Micole, who hadn't been around after she transferred to a high school for pregnant and parenting teens, came and brought her baby girl. Linda was there, wildin' out as usual. She had also dropped her load. She named him TJ, (Tyson Jr.). Jurnee's uncle was working the grill, so the food was bangin'. The music was blastin' out classic hits, song after song. Foxy Brown's lyrics, *'Ain't no nigga like the one J got'* screamed from the speakers as Jigga backed her up. I was flowing like I wrote the damn song. I made the center of the green grass my dance floor. After that, everybody did the same. We were getting our party on! People were singing along with me, "...keeps me in diamonds and leather; sleeps around but he gives me a lot, friends are telling me I should leave him alone... tell them freaks to find a man of their own." Linda was feelin' it; she was starting to love the party scene too much. I guess she felt this song 'cause it was tailored to her situation. Her man kept her with money in her pocket and fresh new shoes on her *and* her son's feet. She even had some nice sized diamond studs in her ears. That was the shit to us young girls then. A pair of Air Max and an outfit to match... *shiiit,* that meant a nigga had mad love for you. 'A coke and a smile' is what my mother called it. Linda's baby daddy, Tyson (despite taking care of home), was a straight up ho. Word was – he kept pussy on his breath. He was a young dope dealer caught out there. Shit, most of the young niggas were especially the ones from our hood. JJ was and so was Jurnee's boyfriend, Kevin. Well, that's before, Kevin got hemmed up by the police. Thank God, he never put it out there he was fucking my mother. That would have been the ultimate humiliation. I knew I recognized the nigga. I had only seen him up close a few times, once before when he picked up Jurnee, another time at the club and the last time at my house. I don't know if it dawned on him that he was fuckin' his girl's best friend's mother. If he did, the nigga was probably poppin' his collar thinking he's a mackdaddy. I recognized that arrogant bop that he had when he came out the bedroom of our house, the moment he stepped out his ride. What did Tracy B get out of fuckin' a young boy besides a wet ass? Stella Got Her Groove back got the oldheads thinking they can do that shit, but that's trife. What kind of example are you setting for your sons and daughters? Tracy B should have thought about that shit! At the barbeque most of the hustlers pulled up in flashy whips, painted up like 'candy' with shiny rims and beatin' music. That's why niggas couldn't wait until it got hot outside. In the summer, they wanted to stunt with their new toys they hustled and saved all winter for. They were all complimenting each other's rides, competing secretly. JJ had a gold Delta '88 on chrome with one big ass speaker in the back. I was proud because I was now his woman and no longer the virgin of the crew. Yep, I eventually gave up the golden pussy. So, I was lost in love with the man that 'popped my cherry.' He was looking good that day as usual. He had on his fresh white Air Force Ones that we called, 'dookies' in the hood. He was rockin' a pair of Polo shorts, with a fresh new Polo shirt on, smelling delicious. Before he joined the crowd, he walked toward the alley where some other young hot boys had a gambling' game going. He acknowledged me by smiling my way.

"Hey, baby."

"What's up, cutie?" I joked. "Where's your woman? Wherever she at, she better come get you before you get snatched up... lookin' all good out here." We loved to tease one another. "Damn, you lookin' all brand new." (Meaning he had on new clothes and shoes.) Knowing me like he did, he stopped me before I could finish.

"Don't trip. I got yo' shit in the trunk... a 4 ½ in boys, right?" I smiled, "Damn, I love that nigga." My mother concluded perfectly, '*a coke and a smile.*' I thought. JJ went to his car, got my shit and then went to get his gamble on.

Everyone was enjoying the atmosphere. Some fast paced music was thumpin' out the sound system. I don't even remember what it was; I just remember seeing Linda breaking it down as she always did. She was out there molesting herself, dancing like she was getting paid. It was rumored that she was now a full time stripper. Jurnee's grandma came out the house and stopped her show. "Girl, save something for the imagination." Linda laughed. She was high (again). The barbeque was fine until this guy pulled up in a drop top Eldorado sittin' on 20's. Every female there was ready to fuck his car. He was cute too...another well-known playa on the rise. His name was Rilow and he was *this* summer's buzz. He sat in his car bumpin' Master P's – '*This is for the bourbons and Cadillac's.*' His music drowned out our little backyard stereo; everyone was looking in his direction. Everybody spoke to him. A couple of girls almost broke their necks trying to get his attention. Then, *POP! POP! POP!* Out of nowhere, somebody started shooting. Everybody started dropping to the ground, screaming. Rilow got ghost, as did everyone else. We never saw it coming. Come to think about it, we never did find out who the shooter was. Good thing, no one was hurt. But that scab ruined our barbeque, bringing the heat, messing up our good

54

time. It always that one nigga that fucks it up for the rest of us!

Chapter Six

Senior year in high school was the year. It came – it went. Everything happened so fast. My mother decided to move to California to help take care of her sick mother, Grandma Shirley. There was no way I was leaving. I had made the Miltown my nesting place. I hardly ever visited Chicago or spoke to the people I knew when I lived there. Milwaukee was my home now. Maraca had an apartment in the projects. She was 19, already. I would be eighteen this year, so I moved in with her and my niece. She was almost 2, such a pretty little fat girl, but mischievous – my niece Mariah Ashley was a number. Everybody loved her spoiled ass. After a while Tracy B sent for her grandbaby to come live in California with her and Austin. My sister let her go. Mariah was so excited; I remember the day so clearly.

"I moving to Cal-e-forna with my Nana, so I can swim everyday and she gon' take me to mittymouse house... Tee-Tee, you wanna go?" I smiled at this little person who always made me feel special.

"No, little momma, but tell Mickey Mouse I said, "hi" and send me a picture of his house."

"I going back to Cali, to Cali; nah I don't think so." She quoted Notorious BIG's remake of

LL Cool J's, Going Back to Cali. We all busted out laughing at 'Ms. Personality'; a little grown 2 year old, going on 21.

That left Maraca and I (now project bunnies) in the two-bedroom apartment...in the projects. She had her boyfriend, and I had a few, myself. I was hot in the ass, but responsible and self disciplined. JJ was still my main nigga, but I had a little extra on the side. He had jeopardized our bond by going out and making a baby on me! That incited baby momma drama and I was not trying to be the star of that sitcom. He was my first love and of course, I still had feelings for him. That nigga was my kryptonite. He would always be that nigga to me! It took me awhile to shake the hurt, (that's why I started creepin), but I was ready with open arms when he begged to get back, like a fool allowing him to undo the damage that was already done, just to do it again. How could I not accept him back? That nigga popped my cherry and had the first dick I ever sucked. That just made me go to Planned Parenthood and get on birth control. I requested depo - a shot given every three months to avoid pregnancy.

I went to school everyday, although I began to slack in the athletic department. I was growing out of that stage. I felt like there were too many other things I could do after school, at least that's what I thought. We were approaching the middle of the school year and my counselor, the short fat man, Mr. Lynn, was on all the seniors about future plans. By his appearance you would think he was half man, half pig. He wore glasses and had a huge overbite. He talked like he was holding his nose and breathed like he was asleep. Just being in his presence was aggravating enough for me, so I immediately gave off an '*I don't give a fuck attitude*'; just to get out of there. Time had come so fast, it's like one day I woke up and I was a senior. I hadn't even planned for life after high school graduation. I was living day-to-day. Now, here it was my turn to visit his office and I didn't know what to say. The window outside of his office was covered with other senior's acceptance letters from colleges and universities from all over - Howard, Yale, Hawaii Pacific, TSU, Spellman, FAMU, UCLA.... all over the world. *Dear Prospective Student: I am pleased to inform you of our acceptance to our prestigious college. Some read, our university is proud to welcome you to our family.* I was in disbelief, even Travis Rowe, the kid in LD (the learning disability class) was accepted to MATC, Milwaukee Area Technical College. What the hell was I thinking? I hadn't even applied to anything at this point. Wait, I did... Lane College in Jackson, Tennessee, where Jurnee attended, but I really hadn't given it any serious thought. I just wanted her to stop buggin' so I filled out the application and she mailed it in for me. That's how lax I was about it. Shit, I probably didn't even give a return address, that's how nonchalant I was about the situation. Mr. Lynn read my posture and got straight to the point.

"Miss Blair, why haven't you applied to any colleges?"

"Because... I don't want to."

"With just a high school diploma, you won't qualify for a lot of the high paying jobs."

"Oh, well."

"With an attitude like that, you won't make it very far. That cute little face may have helped you through high school, but not in the real world, girlie."

"You don't know me."

"No, but I know a lot of others with that same attitude."

"Oh well."

"Well, since you don't want to hear it, no need in me wasting your time and my energy. I can already predict where you're headed." He cut me off before I could finish, "Do you know how to speak Pig Latin?"

"What? What the hell does that have to do with anything?"

"Do you, smarty-pants?"

"No," I snapped.

"Funny... most do. Anyway, here's to your future, Farewell!"

"What? Are you crazy or something, mental?" He just smiled sheepishly. "Farewell. Shit... bye to you too!" I threw back at him. Jerk! I walked out and slammed the door. That was some dumb shit. That was weird to me, in the middle of our conversation, he wanted to know if I understand Pig Latin and when I told him no, he says... farewell? Then it hit me like a Mack truck. I stopped right in my tracks and cursed, *"That porky mothafucka!"* He just played me. He said he knew where I was headed. That cock sucka said 'farewell' – meaning 'welfare' in Pig Latin. His fat, stank ass just said I'm headed straight for welfare and thought that bullshit was funny. Fuck him!

Chapter Seven

Graduation was gradually approaching. We had senior polls. I got best dressed, of course, most popular, biggest flirt and biggest playa (stereotype). Maria, from my part-time crew, got best hair and the rest was left for the geeks. You know... most likely to succeed, most likely to be principal of the school, best smile, and all that other tired bullshit. I still hung with my square crew occasionally. They didn't like to do anything but go to the movies, bowling, and lame shit like that. During one of our corny outings, Maria invited this chic named, Savanna. She went to a private high school in the suburbs. She liked to kick it, like I did, so we clicked immediately. I hooked her up with JJ's cousin, Marell, and we all went to the Sybris Suites for my birthday. We partied like we were bringing a New Year in. JJ bought me a tennis bracelet and some gold hoop earrings. Marell brought the Moet and weed; and we got bent. I don't even like to drink, but JJ insisted that I party with them and stop acting like I couldn't hang. I fixed his ass; I diluted the Moet with some pineapple juice and damn near drunk the whole bottle. I got really fucked up! When Marell pushed Savanna in the pool, the water fight began! That shit was bananas. I'll admit that was on some big kid shit, but it felt good to let my hair down.

After awhile, JJ and I slipped off to the steam room and he gave me my real birthday present. He ate my pussy for the first time. He didn't know what he was doing, but I was happy my baby was maturing off that, *"J am not gon' eat nothing that's gon' get up and walk away,"* shit. He had me moaning like crazy from the slightest touch of his tongue. My imagination was going crazy. He came up off the kitten and I returned his favor. I had definitely gotten better at it. The nigga had me practicing enough. I was moaning, putting the vibration on that dick. I had his toes curling and that made me do it even longer. He pulled me on top of him and slid his Mandingo right in. All right, it wasn't a Mandingo, but it wasn't a little willy either; it was fitting for my trap. I didn't care if Savanna and Marell heard me. They probably didn't, because the radio was so loud.

"JJ, I love you, boy."

"I love you too, bay."

"Why can't you do right by me then?"

"I can, bay. We gon' be together forever; you mine."

"You promise?"

"Didn't I just show you? You gon' have my baby boy, ain't you?"

"Yeah," I lied. That nigga chased too much tail for me to get stuck out there.

"Motley, you better not let me hear nuthin' about you messin' wit' nobody else or I'm gon' fuck you up."

"Don't let me hear shit either, or I'm gon' fuck you and that ho up." We both laughed at that, but I was serious about mine.

"My baby, gangsta!" He bragged.

Chapter Eight

I had to catch the bus to Chicago with my birth certificate, ID, and Social Security card. I had an appointment with a woman named Theresa Pitts from the First National Bank. She had a lot of paper work for me to sign. I had turned the magical age of 18 as daddy would say and was ready to receive the $60,000 Grandma Ethel left me. *Show me the money... Got-damn!!* I was greeted by the receptionist, stated my business and was directed to Ms. Pitt's office.

"Hi. I'm your 2:00 o'clock appointment."

"Hello, young lady. You must be Modesty Blair."

"Yes, I am," I said confidentially, ready to get that check.

"Oh, my. You are so beautiful. Ms. Ethel Smith would be *so* proud of you." I wish she wouldn't have said that, 'cause guilt, shame and sadness consumed me suddenly, all at once. She just didn't know... Grandma wouldn't be so proud of some of the things I was doing.

Ms. Pitts got all the paperwork squared up and just needed my *Jenny Hancock* to seal the deal.

"It was nice to finally meet you, Modesty. Your grandmother bragged about you all the time. Your file is now complete. If you ever need me again, give me a call. Take care, young lady, goodbye." Ms. Pitts had my money wired to the bank branch in Milwaukee. I thought I was getting a check right then and there to cash! It was cool; Chicago was only 1½ hours from Milwaukee.

The ride felt like I was in a paddleboat coasting to China. The bus took forever trying to get back to Milwaukee. My little car had been broke down – the engine went. I was ready to tap into that money. On the ride, I sank into a temporary state of depression in my seat. All I could think about was grandma. I wished Ms. Pitts didn't put her back in the forefront of my mind. Then I got angry with myself, for so many years I blocked out all the memories of grandma to coat my pain. I had too or else I wouldn't have lived in peace. I cried hard the duration of the ride. Afterwards I secretly gave praise to my grandma. *'Thank you, grandma! I love you and even though I don't act like it, I miss you and I'm still your Motley; your baby girl.'*

Chapter Nine

Puff Daddy, Biggie and Mase were right, *The Mo' Money you make, the mo' problems you bring.* I became Ms. Drama Queen overnight. I suddenly had enemies I hadn't met yet. Especially when I got my truck. I purchased a Ford Bronco with some of my money. It was green with the peanut butter top, peanut butter leather seats, with tinted windows. If you didn't read my plates, it probably would have been mistaken for my man's truck. I got personalized plates that read SCHALYD (such a lady). I gave Maraca some money to buy herself a used car. I also paid for the bedroom window I busted out when we got into a fight a few weeks back over some dumb shit (a sister squabble), before housing charged her a hefty maintenance fee to replace it. I flew Tracy, Austin, Grandma Shirley and Mariah back from Cali for my high school graduation. I had to buy extra tickets for graduation because I'd invited so many people. Even though I didn't get any honors, I wanted my family to share this moment with me. I jumped over the first hole that many of them dug for me. They used to gossip so much 'bout – *Modesty is too grown. She gon' end up pregnant. She gon' drop out of school. That girl don't listen to nobody...blah, blah, blah...* I smiled and did my Miss America wave to all of their fake asses. I stopped right before I got to the principal and profiled my Tyra Banks turn like I was on the fashion runway. Everybody was hollering for me, *'Go on girl! Watch out now! Modesty, you are a trip. That's my baby up there. That's my cousin. That's my niece.'* My family was so ghetto and indeed showing out! I couldn't wait to shed that cap and gown to show off my new mini Coogi dress. It was cream with a lot of different pastel colors in it, soft pink, purple and green. It was the shit. I wore pink open toed, Enzo stiletto sandals. Couldn't nobody tell me nothin'... I was flossin'. Tracy B said my name should have been 'Cocky' that night, not Modesty.

After graduation, the school had a reception in the cafeteria. Everybody met up in there. Somebody was missing though.

"Where's JJ?" my voice cracked when I finally realized her wasn't present. Nobody said anything. "Hello! Am I talking to anybody?"

"He didn't come; you said I would meet Uncle JJ when I got here." Mariah whined.

"Shut up!... and he ain't your uncle."

"You said it, Auntie," she snapped back with her grown-ass talking smart.

I was embarrassed. My nigga didn't even show up and he didn't even try to page me. I know my feelings were bruised more than anything.

"So what y'all want to do now?" I faked my joy, changing the subject and trying to play it off.

"It's up to you, Motley. It's your day," Tracy B acknowledged.

"Well since everybody already ate, I think I'll go to the graduation party my friend is having and catch up to y'all later." I tried to brush them off, but they wanted to take photos to savor the moment. After what seemed like a thousand snapshots, we finally went separate ways. I went straight to JJ's momma's house. Butterflies filled my stomach when I hit the corner. He wasn't there. I blew his pager and cell phone up. He didn't answer either of them; I was heated. If I was a cartoon character, steam would be coming from my nose and fire would be flying out of my ears. I called his cell phone again to listen to his voice mail messages. I knew the code 'cause the phone was in my name and I was the one to set up his mailbox.

"Wuz-zup, for all y'all ho's calling my man, hang up and don't call again. For the niggas, leave a message and I might tell him, you called." I smiled listening to my recording. He couldn't change it either 'cause I wouldn't give him the code. So, he tried to answer the phone every time it rang. But when he missed it, I swear most people left messages, especially for me to hear; so I guessed they knew I checked them. I pressed pound to access the mailbox.

You have 3 new messages:

Message 1 - "Hey man, get that ho off your answering machine and get at me, one!!"

Message 2 - "Bitch please, yo' man ain't tell me don't call no more until he does, I'm still calling."

Message 3 - "Hey, baby! What's taking you so long? You better not be with that little girl on your machine. She sounds too immature for you anyway. Grow up chic... and hurry up, JJ!"

That message got my attention; I pressed #6 to call back the number right back.

"Hello." It was the woman's voice.

"Who the fuck is this?" I demanded an answer.

"*Excuse me?*" She said, with much attitude like she was the one offended.

"Is my man JJ with you, trick?" I shouted.

"Look little girl, don't call disrespecting me. Call your man!" *Click!* I heard the dial tone.

I called back until she finally answered again.

"What?... shit! You'se a crazy little bitch," she snapped.

"Ho! You don't know me! Where the fuck you at? I'll show yo' ass crazy."

"Lil' girl, don't be no fool! You don't know me."

"Just tell me where you live then?" I challenged her. She shouted an address. I don't know exactly what she said, I just heard 55th and Center and I hung up. I was on my way. I was so hot I didn't know what would happen when I got there, I just knew I was gonna blackout on that bitch. I didn't remember the address, so I rode down 55th and Center until I spotted JJ's car... and I did. That bastard was pulling off. I chased behind him furiously. I didn't get to see the house he came out of, or the woman. But I'm sure she saw my truck, so we would meet soon enough. JJ was driving like a bat out of hell and

I was right behind him in hot pursuit. He dipped in an alley, hit a corner and I lost him. He better be lucky he did. I was so upset I probably would have done something I would have regretted later... for real. I blew up his phone and pager again. I even rode down 55th again. It was no use; I had no luck finding him. I retired my 007 hunt and went the hell home. Thank God nobody was there. They were still savoring my accomplishment. That mothafuck'n JJ ruined day. That night, I cried myself to sleep.

As soon as I woke up the next morning, I didn't even call him. I called the cell phone company and got his cell phone disconnected. Fuck him! I knew the summer was gonna be off the hook and I was single too... I went from tennis 'shoe princess' to 'stiletto queen.' They accented my track star legs much better than Air Ones – and I was lovin' the look. My shorts had to be thigh high for me to even put them on. I had a whole new wardrobe and a new look. I got my hair cut shorter; I went with the Halle Berry look. It was all about me. I was the city's newest and youngest hot girl once more and my name was buzzin' and I was lovin' that too. Savanna and I had grown closer. Jurnee didn't even come home for the summer after her freshman year in college. She stayed in Jackson, TN for summer school. So now, Savannah and me were new hangin' partna's. Jurnee and I basically had phone visits. We would talk for hours at a time, catching up on the dirt. Although, we didn't seem as close, she was still my girl.

Leaving the house to get in the groove of things, I dipped into a car wash bumpin',' 'Niggas Ain't Shit but Ho's and Tricks',' by Trina and almost flipped my truck over trying to show off. But, I didn't care 'cause I got everybody's attention and I couldn't wait to jump out looking fly on they asses! This was the hot boys and balla's car wash. I was bound to catch some action of action. The car wash was right on the corner of 26th and Capitol, in the hood where I liked it and you didn't dare get your car washed there if it wasn't worth a compliment. I picked Savanna up to roll with me. We were the center of attention on sight. Savanna was lighter than I was, just a little bit taller, and had thick black hair just above her shoulder. She brought a lot of attention to herself 'cause she had big ta-tas and big legs. Men loved her thick ass.

This player walked up spittin' game, "Wuz up, Savanna? Who's ya girl?"

"Hey, Dillon... This is Modesty, Modesty this is Dillon."

"What's up, Red? I like you." Dillon looked like he was from down south. He had gold teeth and a deep southern accent. "What y'all doing when y'all leave here?" His 'here' sounded like 'her.'

"Why? You want to take us out?" I was picking up on my game.

"Not 'us', Lil momma... you." I was feelin' this nigga already 'cause he was so up front (and not counting he was chocolate, just like I liked 'em.) We exchanged numbers.

71

"What's your address? I'm comin' over there later just in case I need to find you. I'm not letting you slip away. You gon' be mine." *Dayum,* he was aggressive too. For some reason I found that attractive. As soon as he walked away, Savanna gave me the scoop on him.

"Gurl, where you know him from?" I quizzed.

"From the eastside. He lives down the street from Maria's house. Girl, he's crazy. The first day I met him, he checked this nigga Maria was dealing with named, Maine for putting his hands on her. Can you believe that big ass nigga, Maine, bowed down to Dillon and stayed in his place? Dillon told him, *'fuck with my little cuz again and I'll do more than confront yo ass.'* I bet Maine didn't. Girl, don't nobody fuck with Dillon like that. He's got a rep!"

"For real? He's cute though," I blushed.

"Hell yeah he is and he got some change too. That's his pink and burgundy Monte Carlo. He calls it, *Pink Passion.*" Savanna said, pointing to his car. His shit was tight. Nice and detailed, hand washed to perfection.

"Why you ain't ever hook up with him then?"

"Girl, please. I heard he a woman beater and he's a wanna be pimp. He think he got ho's working for him. That's outta my league."

"Damn, he like that?"

"Uh huh."

"Why'd you put him on me then?"

"Shit, I wasn't about to hate on him in his face. He the type of nigga that will 'pop a ho' in the mouth. He wasn't about to embarrass me, shiiit!"

"So, I shouldn't talk to him?" I asked, confused.

"Hell naw... but it's on you. If you do, don't think you can talk slick to him 'cause you got a sassy mouth. He ain't hearing it," she warned. Me being the person I was, I had all intentions on giving this nigga some play. I'll just work my shit and let my punanny work a mojoe on his ass.

My truck was ready. Detailed to the 'T'. We jetted down to the lake to style and profile. The strip was jumpin'. Freak Nic traffic, it was a big ass car and fashion show. Some troll-looking hoodrats approached me. It was about 4 of them. The ugliest troll did all the yapping.

"Which one of y'all is Modesty?"

"Why do you want to know?" I spoke up.

"If you're Modesty, then you'll find out."

The tall skinny bird with them said, "That's her." Then the ugliest broad pointed saying, "This is my sister Sabrina. You called, disrespecting her and had the nerve to roll through her block? She's pregnant and too old to fight yo' little ass, but I'm gone settle this shit right now."

One of the back round trolls said, "Fire on that bitch!" The gruesome bitch hit me right in my face. We went right there in the parking lot and right away there was a crowd. I was warming her ass up. I knew I was, cause the tall skinny chick caught a lapse of memory, forgot she was pregnant and tried to get some free licks in. I knocked the ugly bitch down and charged for the skinny bitch. The other trolls were like, "You better not hit her! She's pregnant!"

"The bitch hit me... shit!... her face not pregnant," I yelled at them. I swung and some guy out of the crowd came in the middle of us.

"Y'all go on with that bullshit. Leave this girl alone. I saw y'all come to her wit' that BS... y'all wrong. Go on, and leave her alone." The ugly girl was holding her arm in pain. It looked dislocated. They walked off hollering threats.

"It ain't over. We gon' catch yo' young ass again."

The guy picked up my white Gucci knock-off sunglasses and handed them to me.

"Baby girl, why you here out fighting?" he asked. "You too damn pretty for that."

"I don't even know. Them ho's stepped to me and I'm ain't no punk about mine." I was in raw mode.

"I see you handled yours. They got what they came for. They just hatin' 'cause you doing your thang. You think you gon' be straight?"

"Yeah, I'm all right." I didn't even know him. Every time I seen him after that, he called me 'Lady Tyson'. People I knew were coming up to me. "Damn girl, what was that all about?" "Girl you little ass was throwing 'em." "Savanna scary ass wouldn't be riding wit' me, if I were you." They were right. She hadn't even jumped in the fight. Had it been Jurnee, she would have been in the mix. Why didn't she help me? When my audience cleared up, I snapped at her.

"Why the fuck you let me get jumped?"

"That big girl had some mace and she said if I jumped in she was gonna mace me. You were winning anyway, you didn't need my help." I looked at her like she lost her damn mind and left her fool ass standing right there. I didn't care how she got home.

Chapter Ten

Dillon and I were conversing on a regular basis. He wasn't anything like I thought or he hadn't let that side of him show yet. I could tell he had pimpin' in him 'cause he spoke like one of those players off the Players Ball documentary; real slick, *'yeah ya dig'*, *'understand this'*, *'and recognize'*. His pockets had Benjamins and he had girls on his line 24-7 and he loved to gamble. Even though I knew he was trouble, I got involved anyway. I had an unexplainable attraction to him.

♥ ♥ ♥ ♥ ♥

The summer was still young. Maraca had moved out with her new boyfriend, Skeet, and I was left untamed to be head of the household. Tojoe, Maraca's baby daddy, took me under his wing and treated me like his little sister. He would stop by and check on me every now and then. Sometimes I kept dope for him. Eventually Dillon and Tojoe got acquainted and they started to gamble together in the basement. Gradually they invited more people from both sides and it turned into a crap night... when I would allow it. I was getting $20 a head – that was my house cut. JJ and his little brother even found out and joined in. It felt odd when JJ and Dillon were with me in the same room. JJ wasn't that good at gambling, but his little brother 'Lil Boy' was a baby Gabino. He had a tattoo on his forearm of a pair of dice that read, '*Break Ya'self*'. This nigga was serious on his crap game. He even won a car before. Him and Dillon were two of a kind and they clicked automatically. JJ and I hadn't talked in months; this had to be the longest we'd ever went without talking. One night he made his way up from the gamble and eased his way next to me on the couch.

"Hey stranger," he said.

"Hey," I said dryly.

"Why you get my phone cut off?" he said jokingly.

"Is that all you worried about?"

"Naw, I am worried about you, too. I see you replaced me quick."

"Whatever!" I was nervous because I didn't want Dillon to catch me alone with JJ. I hoped the $1500 I loaned him, would keep him busy. Dillon promised he said he could flip it and give it back with interest. I turned the sound system on and bumped the *Hot Boys*, from the Cash Money Millionaire clique, so it would look like we were just chillin'.

"Oh we can't talk? That nigga got you on lock down like that?"

"Naw... that maggot got you on lock down! She's carrying yo' baby – another baby at that! That's two on me nigga! If you wanna talk about something let's talk about how them trolls jumped me at the lake. How about that?"

"Man, that trick ain't pregnant by me and I checked them broads about steppin' to you like that.

"Checked my ass!! You haven't checked on me. I could've been fucked up!"

"Naw, I heard you handled yours. I know my baby. Motley, you gangsta! I know for sure you can hold your own." I couldn't help but smile. "Yeah, I'm still that down ass bitch." He smiled too and sang, *"Just me and my bitch, just me and my bitch,"* repeating Biggie's classic rhyme. "Girl, you know we Bonnie and Clyde." Right then, he got real serious on my ass. "I miss you, girl. I need you back in my world. Shit ain't been the same without you. We ain't never went this long without talking and you gonna let this country bunkin' ass nigga take my place? That's real fucked up Motley!" I had to admit I was weak for this man. My mind was telling me no, but my heart wouldn't refuse him. Damn, I loved this 'no good ass' nigga.

"Okay, we can talk when all these people leave, but if it gets too late, we gon' do something together tomorrow, a'ight?"

I knew we were going to reconcile; that's why I don't know why I fucked Dillon that night. Nasty, I guess. He fucked like a winner and ate pussy like a champ. Nigga had me running up the wall! He kept pulling me back towards him. "Baby, don't run... take this dick!" I was moaning and hollering like he was killing me, but it felt good. He fucked like he had dope on the dick. After we finished we got in the shower together and laid up talking.

"Why yo' pussy so tight? You a virgin?"

"No, I just haven't been having sex lately."

"Good... 'Cause now that pussy is mine, you hear me?"

"Yeah, I heard you."

"I better not hear about you nowhere fighting over no nigga again. You mine's now." Damn he caught me off guard with that one. I didn't even know he knew about that. "You mine now, ain't you?"

"Yeah," I hyped him up.

"You gone act right?"

"Yeah, baby." I put myself in a bind. *Damn, Modesty... what did you get yourself in to this time?* I thought to myself. I avoided JJ for a whole week before he finally caught up to me.

"Dag, baby you hidin' from me? If you don't want to fuck wit' a nigga, let me know. It's your choice. If you choose that nigga, I'll step off." I couldn't tell him the truth. "Naw, I've been working everyday for a temp agency." (I didn't even have a job.)

"Ride with me somewhere, so we can talk." I didn't want anybody to see us together, so I told him to meet me at Skeet's house, so I can give Maraca my truck and ride with him. Skeet was mad cool. This was the nigga that taught me how to shoot a gun... and that was on the first night I met him. I hopped in JJ's car feeling paranoid, but then I relaxed 'cause no one could see through his limousine tint. We stopped in the gas station first, for blunts and gas. As soon as he got out, I called Dillon. "Hey, baby. I was just calling to let you know I'm out with Maraca helping her find another car." Her other car had been stolen so, I could pull that off.

"A'ight. How long you gon' be, 'cause I wanna see you later?" It was 4pm and I didn't know what JJ had planned, so I said, "Till about 9pm."

"It don't take that long to find no car."

"My sister is so picky. We'll probably go to every car lot until they're closed."

"You better call me as soon as y'all get back. Naw... as a matter of fact, you call me while y'all searching!"

"Okay, bye." I said, and hung up quick 'cause JJ was walking back to the car. All the shit that I went through with JJ, that nigga still made me feel like I owed him. I was nervous and tried to play if off.

"Boy, I saw you talking to that tramp. You at it already," I laughed.

"Yeah right, she tried to holla, but I told her my woman was in the car and she backed off."

"Don't lie; 'cause I'll go ask a bitch. She went to my high school. Her name is Robin and she's another ho'. She's probably right up your alley with yo' dirty dick!"

"Girl, you still crazy!" We pulled off. He jumped on the highway and I panicked. "Where are we going?"

"Damn, calm down. Don't worry I'm going to have you back in time to check in with that fuck nigga."

"Naw, it ain't like that. I told Maraca I would go to the mall with her before it closed." Maraca was my alibi for the day. "Y'all can go tomorrow. I'm kidnapping you for the day," he smiled suspiciously. Damn, now I had to think of another lie to tell Dillon. The more I lied, the better I got at it. JJ took me to Great America in Gurnee, IL. It was about an hour away. We kicked it all day. He won me two big teddy bears, a huge Tweety and a bear with a clown suit on. Afterwards we went to Red Lobster to eat and then got a room in Gurnee. I had forgotten to check in with Dillon. I would have to figure out something to tell him, when I got home. JJ rolled up a blunt and we smoked it just like the good ole' days. I couldn't shake JJ and didn't want too, regardless of our past. We fucked like rabbits for the rest of the night, like this was our last night together. Guess that was enough to put us back on good terms 'cause the next morning when he dropped me off he said, "I love you. I'll call you after I handle this business. When you get time, call and book us a cabin for the weekend in Wisconsin Dells." He handed me a $100 bill, "Go get a swimsuit."

I had gotten myself in a helluva mess! As soon as I walked in the house, Skeet was slouched on the living room couch playing Madden on Play station. He said, "Dillon been looking all over for ya' ass."

"Shit!!... What did you tell him?"

"I told him I hadn't seen you or Maraca all morning."

"Where's Maraca?" I panicked, worrying about getting out of this jam with Dillon.

"At work," he replied, still engrossed in his game.

"So he thinks I'm with Maraca?"

"I guess. I didn't get into if you were or weren't. I just said I hadn't seen either one of y'all all morning."

"Oh, good lookin' out," I thanked him.

"Don't get me mixed up in your mess. I don't want any parts of that conniving shit."

"Cool, just do me one favor."

"Hell naw!"

"It ain't nothin' you gotta be in. Damn, can you just drop me off?"

"I'm busy. Your truck is out there, Maraca left the keys."

"I know but I don't wanna drive, please Skeeter." I put on my little girl voice and puppy-dogface.

"Where you tryin' to go?"

"To the emergency room at the hospital."

"I'm not even gonna ask." He put the game on hold, nodded his head and got his keys. "Modesty, you'se a mess if I've ever seen one." I just smiled.

I checked myself into Sinai Hospital. I told them I was having strong migraines and blurred vision. They gave me a wristband and did all the usual paperwork. I got a cat scan to check for internal problems; of course they didn't find anything. So they prescribed some pain pills and released me. I did have migraines occasionally, so it wasn't a total scam. I went to the extreme to get outta this mess... it worked though! I called Dillon from the hospital.

"Speak."

"Hey, it's Modesty," I whispered.

"Where the fuck you been?" His voice was filled with venom.

"Before you curse me out, can you come and get me?"

"Fuck you. Stay where you been. I know you was wit' some nigga. Have him come get you. Or, did he leave yo' ass stranded?"

"Listen, you got it all wrong. I'm at the hospital. I got dropped off last night because I couldn't drive."

"Hospital? What happened to you? What hospital?" His voice changed to concern. I had defused the beast.

"I felt faint, that's all. I'm at Sinai Samaritan on Wisconsin."

"Don't play with me Modesty. I'll holla at chu' when I get there." I played my bullshit game about being sick and he pampered me for the rest of the night. My scam worked. I was out of the doghouse and he was clueless that I was with JJ.

"Baby, you had a nigga heated, looking for yo' ass. I know I like yo' lil yellow ass 'cause I don't run up behind no bitch and you had me open last night...but the shit better not happen no mo'!" That was my clue – I was swimming in dangerous waters.

"Why I gotta be a bitch?"

"You know what I mean." He looked so serious. He scared me.

"I know," I played it cool.

"Next time, call me, and if you can't - have somebody else call me. Don't make a nigga crazy like that no mo'. Shit is psycho out here nowadays. I have to be able to trust you. If I can't trust you, ain't no need for you to be around."

I felt a tad bit guilty about my overnight rendezvous with JJ. I needed to choose one of them before this shit got too complicated. But, what the fuck? Men live double lives all the time. Why couldn't I?

Chapter Eleven

Tojoe, Maraca's baby daddy, called me up talkin' 'bout he needed to talk to me about something. Him and Trey, his road dawg, stopped over before they went to the outlet mall in Kenosha. He put a bug in my ear about the word on the street, concerning me.

"Yo Modesty, some shiesty niggas got word of the major paper that's being thrown during your late night gambles. Niggas are planning to run up in the next session to make a come up. They ain't playin' either. They talkin' 'bout robbing everybody up in that bitch... including you! They think you dibbling in the game."

"Damn, niggas out here starving like that, that they wanna rob a female? Well, dayum!"

"Yup, and a nigga would flip if something happened to you, Modesty. A brother got love for you for real. You like blood to me. I got to apologize, 'cause the rumor about you dealing is probably my fault. Remember that day I had my runner pick up some sack from you? He probably ran his mouth and let out the wrong information. You know niggas gossip worse than bitches."

"So what should I do, Tojoe?"

"Nothing...what can you do? You can't stop something that hasn't happened yet. Just be careful and slow up all that traffic you have in and out of there – that means no more gambles. I'll keep my work at my girl's house and you watch your back. Don't trust everybody you keep company with. Everybody that smile at you, or know your name, ain't your friend. I got a lil 22', you can keep in the house just in case. Don't carry it around with you – not in your purse or in your car. And, don't show it off and definitely don't play with it. It's not a toy. You know about the safety lock, bullets, and cocking it?"

"Yeah, Skeet taught me."

"Who?"

"Oh, umm... never mind." I said, not wanting to throw Maraca's new man in his face.

"You'll be straight. I don't want to scare you. I just want you to be safe, than sorry," he said with concern. He must have sensed the fear or read the look on, my face. "Sorry shaw-ty, did I spook you?"

"Naw, I'm cool wit' my 22. I'll call her Peggy Sue," I said jokingly. "Thanks, bro," I stated, as I admired my new comrade - silver with the pearl white handle. Perfect fit for my make-up bag. I slipped the small handgun under the sofa cushion and walked with Tojoe towards the door.

"Why didn't you ask me to go to the outlet? You know that shopping is my natural high...my therapy," I stated, knowing it was an open invite.

Trey rolled a few blunts for the highway and I kicked it like I was one of the homies. We hit the e-way (express way) and splurged out at the outlet. I treated myself with a new pair of BCBG sandals, some fitted Versace pants and a Coach belt. I picked up some stuff to send to Cali for my little boo, Mariah. What the hell, I even grabbed

Dillon a Nautica fit and felt like a trickin' nigga try'na butter up his girl.

Later that night Dillon and I caught the midnight flick at Mill Road Theater. There, we ran into Linda, my girl from high school. We had completely lost touch.

"Linda, hey gurl, where you been? I ain't seen you in a minute?"

"Modesty! Oh, my God! Gurl, look at your hair! You done cut it all off. It fits you though." We gave each other a big hug. She had a wig on that was too big for her head. She looked so hoed out. I heard she was heavy in the strip game now, doing unmentionable things. That party scene wore her ass down fast! Of course I wasn't about to question it. I hadn't seen her in almost a year; that would've been ill mannered.

"Give me your number, so I can call you," I said, excited to see her.

"I don't have a number. Give me yours and I'll call you when I get around a phone," she said embarrassed. She didn't need to be. It was only me – she still was my girl. She looked like she needed another hug, so I gave her a tight squeeze and said, "I love you, girl." Things were not always right in people's lives. So I gave Linda a little assurance and told her, "I'm here for you if you need me."

Surprisingly, Linda called the very next day taking me up on that pronto. She needed an escape. We started back hanging out and things were just like our high school days. She had convinced me to let her and her son TJ, move in with me, to get back on her feet. I threw her a couple hundreds to help her get a jump-start. It was only money and then, I was still in the plus and besides... she was still my girl. Who gave a fuck where Tyson was?

One night we were chillin' out, smoking and drinking and I don't know if the weed had her emotional or it was the liquor that made her do it. Or maybe, she needed to exhale, but she started pouring her heart out.

"Modesty, you got it made gurl. That lil' shit you complain about... the shit you consider problems... gurl, I would love for mine to be that simple. You ain't got no kids. You got a ride, your own place and your money is straight." I sat listening as the chemicals set in our bloodstream. "I didn't graduate. I was supposed to walk across that stage with you. Gurl, I heard you clowned them. I missed that shit! I didn't get a chance to do that. I messed up. I fucked up my whole life, all on account of a man. And, he ain't even here to help me. He promised me, he would never leave me... I had a baby for that nigga. I thought that meant something and look what happened? He called his self cheatin' and messin' with a grimy ho and the bitch set him up on some stick-up shit for her brother and got him killed! He died doggin' my ass out and look at me... I would still be wit' his ass. I knew all that nigga dirt. I guess that's what they mean by 'til death do us part. I bet he in hell somewhere laughing at my ass. Gurl, promise me... don't ever let the 'good' dick make you foolish." Well, that answered my question...

Tyson was dead and gone – damn shame! Linda started laughing deliriously. "Yeah nigga, you played me," she was talking to the air. Then, came the stream of tears. "That mothafucka' ain't leave me and my baby shit! A bitch gotta do what a bitch gotta do, to feed us. Me!... by myself!! Damn, Modesty; don't ever do this to ya'self. Don't ever think havin' a baby by a nigga gon' change somethin'. That's some bogus shit. I need to beat the bitch that made that shit up! It ain't gon' make him act right, love you more or even stay wit' yo ass. His mind is already made up what he gon' do... stay or leave... love you or use you. A nigga is gon' do what he gon' do regardless. So, just do you!" She cried loud, like a baby with no shame. I was lost for words. Man that was deep. She cried so hard, that I wept with her and guaranteed, "As long as I have a place to stay, so do you. As long as I got money, so do you. You don't have to hurt no more... you home. I got you." She got me so depressed. I was thinking about everything that ever happened to me. Shit, I was crying about shit that happened when I was a kid. I was crying about grandma. I was crying about daddy. Hell, I even cried about JJ missing my graduation. I had to clear my head and think about something else, so I called Dillon to come over and put me to sleep...and daddy came and rocked his baby. The next morning he called me up. "Damn, girl. Was you mad at me last night?"

"Naw, why you say that?"

"'Cause you were scratching the shit out of me. I got train tracks all across my ass."

Chapter Twelve

Just when I thought things were all good, some basket case female spray-painted *'Charge it to the game'* in gold spray paint, across my shiny, green truck. For days, I couldn't figure out who it was until the phone calls began.

"Find ya' own man, bitch. He's only fucking wit' your ass 'cause you paying: You so stupid. He gon' break yo ass. It's all good ho – keep givin' up the duckets!"

I kept receiving mental ass messages from this mysterious broad. I couldn't figure out who or what they were talking about because I was friends with a few dudes. Mainly Dillon and JJ, but I couldn't narrow down which one of them had a deranged ho' on their hands. Shit, then I thought, it couldn'a been JJ because I was his deranged ho, ain't nobody flip the script on me! The answer came a week later. This bird-looking ass girl pulled up on the side of my truck, pushing Dillon's Monte Carlo. Seriously, at first I didn't even notice until she started laughing out loud and hollering, "I see you charged a new paint job to the game, trick." It dawned on me quick that it was the same crazy broad that called herself, fucking up my car.

"Naw, I charged it to Dillon ho'," I fired back.

"Don't fake it! He already told me you paying him. You fool-ass bitch!" She screamed out the window.

We were actually riding down the street arguing through the window.

"Don't get it twisted," I snapped back.

"Naw, you got it twisted. You see who pushin' the ride - me, the wifey, his woman, you stupid ho'!"

"Bitch, I got my own. That's why.... please believe, if need be, I'd be pushin' his whip."

The driver behind her blew the horn, 'cause we were holding up traffic. Otherwise, we would have gone back and forth until one of us got tired. It didn't matter 'cause she called my phone to continue the argument.

"How in the hell did you get my number?"

"He gave it to me."

"Yeah, right."

"He also told me where you live and you gave him $1,500 trick ho."

"I didn't give him shit."

"You really thought he would wife you when you fucking everybody in the city? He pulling you along on a string letting you think you doing something slick. Oh, and for the record, he knows you still fucking that nigga JJ."

I hung up and turned the power off on my phone. This bitch knew too much, something was up. First of all, I didn't *give* Dillon anything, I loaned him $1,500. He flipped it, just like he said he would, but I didn't get the interest he promised. But, where could she have gotten the information about me messing with JJ from? That's right!... He had been hanging tough with Lil Boy, JJ's little brother. That punk snitch! I went home to get my thoughts together. Linda had company; some guy she had just met named Bennie Swan. He was leaving when I got there. She said he was a potential trick. She planned to have him paying her major loot if she played her cards right. I searched for Peggy Sue, my little 22', as Linda let her guest out. I figured I might need it if haters continued to stalk me. My cohort was nowhere to be found, I excused it as me being too anxious and decided to search for it later. I told Linda to spark one so I could clear my mind and analyze things. JJ had turned me into a straight weed junkie. I told her about my drama and mellowed out. I got horny, as I usually did when I smoked, so I called JJ. We managed to maintain common grounds. We were not together, but we hooked up anytime he wanted or anytime I wanted. He didn't question what I did and I didn't question him. I hoped when I talked to him, Lil Boy didn't put anything in his ear about Dillon. *Ugh*, Dillon, I was trying not to think about him. I hadn't even talked to him yet and I didn't plan to until I got my information right. I didn't want to deal with that yet. One thing for sure - Dillon was telling my business, cause his ho knew too much to be bluffing me. My thoughts rested on my temporary antidote - some good dick.

JJ answered on the first ring. "Hey, Motley. I was wondering when you were gonna call. I just left a message on your cell. Your voice mail came on after the first ring." His voice alone soothed my soul. "My battery died. I need to see you. Can you come over?" I whined.

"Yeah, give me thirty minutes. Let me handle something and I'll be there."

"A'ight."

Regardless of the situation or our status, JJ always made me feel relaxed and comforted. He hit me off just right that night. I knew I still loved that nigga! No matter how many times I lead him astray, his dog ass kept finding his way back home.

Chapter Thirteen

The summer was winding down. Savanna and I were back on speaking terms due to my kind heart. I didn't hold a grudge. Dillon and I broke it off because his girlfriend kept stalking me. JJ and I decided we were meant to be together and got back together (again). I figured no one else could put up with me, but him. I was wild and he was the only nigga in the hood that could tame my kitty. Linda had moved out; we weren't speaking because her potential 'cake daddy' came at me at a pool party. I told her about it and she told me, "Break his ass, get him for all you can," her exact words. "It's enough to go around, let 'em trick," she stressed. Evidently I ran my mouthpiece better than she did, 'cause I had his ass buying appliances and some more shit. She couldn't even get her son pampers. She had fell in love with pimpin'. All that shit she was talking was just, *blah, blah, blah.* She didn't mean any of that tough talk. I guess she was trying to test my loyalty or she didn't want me to know that she had fell for him. In any case, if the dude was off limits, she should have stated that! I hated when females did that shit! If you still feelin' the nigga – say so to avoid unnecessary bullshit! Linda was the one, that told me to come up on this trick and when I did, what did she do? She moved in with her older sister, Georgette, who filled her head up on another level. Where was her sister when she really needed her? All of a sudden Beanie Swan was her man and I slept with him behind her back. For the record – he wasn't her man at the time and I never had sex with him. I have to admit, I let him play with the punanny with his hurricane tongue, but no form of penal penetration was ever conducted. Linda passed the word around town and it was drama when we came in contact with each other. That hurt 'cause I thought we were better than that. Was I wrong to think that? We could've handled the situation between us. Instead we had everybody else's input and some extra shit to the story. The final outcome – I had to beat her older sister down with a bat.

One day, JJ and I were sitting in my truck at the corner store and Georgette, Linda's older sister pulled up. She was at least 25 with two rug rats. She was medium height and heavy set. She had life and bullshit all mixed up – It was all fucked up! She really thought I was going to let her smack me. She pulled up with her children in the back seat of the car.

"Wuz up, Modesty?" She said, real shitty.

"Wuz up?" I gave it back to her.

"What's all this shit about you talking bad about my sister and my nephew?"

"What!" I snapped back.

"Yeah, you involving my nephew, I know so'em," she said trying to start of fight.

"That doesn't make since, and anyway he's a child. He can't even defend his self. Why the hell would I talk bad about a baby? If anything I said Linda need to take care of her baby and stop running behind these niggas." That bitch wanted to hit me so bad, and this was her cue.

"Don't get fuckin' smart... I'll smack yo' ass."

Honestly, I wasn't getting smart, but I wasn't no punk either. "You not gon' smack shit. I gritted back."

Georgette parked her car and boldly marched up to my driving window where I was sitting and whacked the shit out of me. I was stunned at her audacity. All hell broke loose. I was trying to drill that fat ho' through the window; at the same time JJ was attempting to pull me to the passenger's side. Georgette headed back to her car like she had accomplished something. I was heated. I know she didn't think I was going out like that. I jumped out with my baseball bat (my hater beater), that I kept in the trunk for the Modesty-haters, and punished that ho'. JJ had to pull me off of her. I felt bad 'cause her kids were hollering and crying, but she should have thought about that before she tried to play *'Captain Save a Ho,'* for Linda's ass. The next night Georgette and three of her girls staked out in front of JJ's house. I just so happened to stop over to see him, but he wasn't home. When I walked back to my truck to leave, they sprung out on me. I hauled ass trying to get back in the house. Them ho's had to have bats and clubs. Ain't no telling what else...I didn't wanna know. I ran back into the house hysterical. JJ's mother and sister ran to my screams. We all went back inside to wait for them to leave. Now I thought I was hard, but I wasn't fucking stupid either... I was out numbered. I knew it was animosity from that night on. I was calling JJ's phone - he wasn't anywhere to be found. He didn't even know about the drama.

In the morning I got up early to handle some business at Planned Parenthood. My coochie felt irritated and I wanted to get the bitch checked out. I thought it was an inflamed yeast infection the way my shit was feeling. Come to find out, I had Chlamydia! The only good thing was that it was curable. I was humiliated and furious with my legs in the stirrups watching the gynecologist send my cultures down to the lab for further testing. I mean it this time, this was the last fuckin' straw that broke the camels back! I'd never had a disease before and it had to be JJ's ass that gave it to me! Dillon would' a been pulled my card if I had given him something. *Damn, J was feeling played, once again!* When the doctor walked out, a nurse came in and asked me the name(s) of my partners. She asked me did I know who I could have gotten Chlamydia from. I felt like an ass for not knowing. I had a clue, but I wasn't 100% sure. She gave me two forms to inform my partner(s) anonymously and told me, they needed to get checked out as well. I filled one out one for Dillon and one for JJ. Irresponsibly, I had sex with both of them with no rubber. Stupid! I had to drink a ½ a cup of some white powdery medicine. It smelled good, like candy, but it was horrible. It tasted like smashed aspirin. It had the worst after taste; I gagged trying to swallow the shit. The nurse handed me a peppermint afterwards. (Was this some sort of incentive for dropping names or a kind gesture?) She advised me not to have sex for two weeks and sent me on my way. I could see the disgust in her eyes like she expected me to come back to see them when I had a more serious disease. But the bitch had me wrong!

Chapter Fourteen

I didn't know who to be mad at other than myself, 'cause I slipped up and let both them niggas go raw. I knew they were both 'fuck-off' kings. *Damn, Modesty! That could have been AIDS.* I huffed out loud to myself. I decided to go to JJ's house and hint around to see if anything was bothering him. Shit, even if he didn't give it to me, I had given it to him, so maybe he would mention some type of hint. I planned the whole conversation out in my head. *"JJ, I felt kind of irritated down there. It could be a yeast infection and if it is, you know I could have given it to you. Men can't get yeast infection, but the bacteria from a woman can 'cause a man to itch or burn, or other symptoms."* He would either name some of his symptoms or he would act like he didn't know what I was talking about. Then, I would have my answer.

It was early; I knew he would be home. I picked up a bag of fruit from one of the Muslim brothas and two bean pies, and like little red riding hood, I was on my way. Regan, JJ's little cousin let me in when I arrived. She was up getting ready for summer school. JJ's momma's house was like a group home. Everybody lived there. Cousins, uncles, friends, - every goddamn body! I got to JJ's door and tried to twist the knob, but it was locked. He had a ghetto ass security lock on the inside of his door. It was a thick-ass shoestring tied from the doorknob, to a small nail sticking out of the wall. I wondered why he had it all conjured up this early in the morning. I peeked through the small opening of the door. I saw four legs at the end of the bed. I couldn't see faces 'cause the door crack wouldn't let me see that far. A pair of dark skinny legs with another pair of light brown female legs crossed over them. My heart raced. I kept trying to make myself believe it wasn't JJ in there. Hell naw! He don't let anybody else sleep in that room. Nobody! So I knew it was his dog ass. I had to get in that room. I eased my frail arm through the crack in the door and undid the shoestring. When I finally got in the room, I stood there stunned... staring in shock not, knowing what to do. JJ must have felt my presence 'cause he woke up. He looked like he saw a ghost.

"What are you doing in here?" He said in shock, he knew he was busted. I immediately attacked him. We tussled in the bed for a few seconds and woke up the girl. JJ somehow got me nailed on the floor. He had the covers wrapped around him and the trick was in her panties and bra. When I saw her face, all my strength raced through me like Popeye when he ate his spinach. I broke loose from JJ and sprung on that ho', bopping her right in the eye. I couldn't believe it! It was the same ho' from the gas station, Robin, the day JJ and I went to Great America. Sneaky bitch – nothing ass nigga!! It was war up in that bitch and I was the commanding General. JJ grabbed for me, I kept dodging his reach and swinging on Robin. Her coward ass wasn't even trying to fight back. She was protecting her face, hollering, "Stop, stop! JJ, please get this crazy bitch." JJ finally grabbed and restrained me. He dragged me into his brother's (Lil Boy), room, butt-ass naked. By this time, we had awoken everybody in the house. I was wildin', especially when I saw JJ's manhood, *my* joy toy, hanging and jangling. I totally lost it! A bitch went berserk!!! The thought of that nasty crab getting all *my* dick and my mind told me to crucify both they asses. His mother came up the stairs with a two by four. When she saw it was us making all the noise, she dropped her equalizer and began to curse.

"Let her go JJ!... and go put some damn clothes on! She isn't gonna do shit. Modesty get the fuck out of my house with that crazy shit, disrespecting my house... get out!"

I just looked at her because I knew the golden rule about not to ever disrespect nobody's mama... at least, not to their face. JJ reluctantly released me. Something he shouldn't have done, 'cause I grabbed the hot iron his little cousin was using before the chaos and threw it at his naked ass with his mother right there. I rushed out, with her cursing at my back.

"Don't ever bring yo' ass back over here, Modesty."

That was it... I had it with JJ's ass. He made me decide to match that nigga and be the 'fuck off' Queen for the rest of the summer. Fuck claiming a man or having one claim me! Being wifey, hurt too badly for me. Wifey is supposed to be the #1 bitch, "numero uno," your main squeeze... the one who gets all the respect, the money and his attention. But in reality, wifey is the one who gets hurt the most. Why do females want to be wifey? When wifey gets the shitty end of the stick! Fuck it! I'll leave that title to another dumb ho' 'cause Modesty Yameyeia Blair is done with it. Fuck you JJ and I mean that shit, nigga!

Chapter Fifteen

The summer was damn near over. I was glad 'cause at least when it starts getting cold, mothafuckas stay in the house and out of everybody else's business. Although Dillon wasn't a fixture in my life anymore, I had a run-in with his punk ass girlfriend, again...the same crab that spray-painted my whip. We had a big brawl right in the middle of Amoco gas station. That nigga Dillon was there, entertained by this shit. Of course, he was rooting for his girl to win. He had a hard on just watching us quarrel.

"Beat her ass...if you don't, I'm gonna beat yours," he was shouting to her.

I wasn't trippin' though. But on the real, we both looked like fools. This nigga was laughing; amused by bitches he'd fucked wit' fighting over his ass. Didn't he look like a big ass pimp, and us, two dumb ho's fighting for Big daddy. After that fight I went home, my body and mind was telling me, no more Modesty! No more drama. I got on my knees and cried to God.

"God please grant me the serenity to accept the things that are unchangeable, and change the things that are unacceptable. Please Lord, send me the answers. In your son, Jesus' name. Amen."

I tried to sleep off the anxiety and drama. I stayed at home in my bed for two days. I can't even remember eating. I had the worst fucking dream. Here I was holding this black ass, hollering ass baby... peeing in my arms, and I'm cursing out JJ. *"My baby need some pampers nigga. What the fuck do I need to do to get child support, police yo' ass?"*

He hollered back, *"Yeah bitch and why you at it, tell the mothafuckas to tell you who yo' baby daddy is, 'cause I ain't the one."*

In my dream, he left. So I called Dillon crying. *"I need some money for this baby."*

He snapped, *"Tramp, you better go get paid all for that good hoing you do and make somethin' happen!"*

I felt small tugs and pulls, I'm like damn, *I know I ain't got a toddler too? Shit!*

I woke up; it was Mariah. Damn, I'm glad that was only a dream. "Save the drama for the baby mommas," I said out loud to myself.

"What you say, tee-tee?" Mariah frowned.

"Nothing... what do you want?"

"Dag, you mean... I should have stayed with Nana. You got some mail, and a lot of people keep calling you; and JJ came over."

"Did you say what I told y'all to say if people asked for me?"

"Yeah, you gone to Chicago for a while and we don't know when you be back."

"Good... gimmie my mail and get out!"

Mariah handed me an envelope and screamed, *"Cruella Deville."* She ran out the room and slammed the door behind her. I was in a bad mood. I would make it up to her later with a dollar or something. The envelope read "Lane College". Damn all the chaos made me forget I had even applied. I ripped the paper right through the envelope:

Dear Prospective Student:
It is my pleasure to welcome you into our prestigious institution for the fall semester. Congratulations on your acceptance!

I didn't even need to read anymore. I hollered so loud, I couldn't stop screaming with excitement. *Yes, God is listening, yes! He understands my cries. Thank you, thank you, I'm saved.* Maraca, Mariah and Skeeter burst into the room. Maraca was now staying back in the house and Skeeter stayed over all the time. My little gambles in the basement and full house of company had been ceased. Even though Skeeter was there to get the news, by now we were not as cool. He called me a little slut ho' because he was salty that I hung out with Tojoe, Maraca's baby daddy. Either that, or he found out I sucked his cousin's dick in the bathroom. But shit... his cousin tricked me. He told me we would do each other and when I finished, he said it was a 69, but he owed me one so, I could call it a 68 and catch him next go round. He left me looking dim-witted and ashamed. In revenge, I got his little nickel and dime spot raided. Yes I did! A scorn bitch will get you back whatever way she can... I knew his whereabouts; it was easy to get at him. Now, we're even. Skeeter disliked me ever since, *I guess.* Oh well... fuck 'em all. I'm going to college niggas!

"Girl, what is wrong with you?" Maraca yelled.

"I got accepted! My ass is outta here. I'm going to college."

Mariah didn't even know what the hell I was talking about, but she started to cheer with me. "Yeeeaaah, my tee-tee going to collish... my tee-tee going to collish!!"

She was hopping around and so was I. We both jumped on the bed, bouncing and cheering. I had to call my girl Jurnee, to tell her the good news. I knew this would be music to her ears. As soon as she heard the news she was ready to plan a campus visit before school started in August. It was already nearing August. I called everybody. Savanna was jealous. I don't know if she thought I was either dumb or not college material. Her response was, "I should apply. I know if you got in, I can too." She tried hard not to sound too offensive, but she was downplaying me. I didn't get offended either. I was glad 'cause the thought of my girl going to college out of state with me made me even more enthused to go.

Jurnee convinced her two uncles to drive us to Tennessee in my truck. I was so excited and ready to shop for school, but I had almost bottomed out of my inheritance. I had splurged so much with my own shopping habits, and trying to take care of everybody, I lost count of my spending. I called JJ to ask for some money for my trip. He agreed to give me $300, but the night before we left, JJ was ghost. Why I thought I could count on him... I don't know. Damn! That's the least he could do! That's why Tracy B always said never put your faith in a man. Thankfully, Jurnee's grandmother gave me $100 for food and a gas card. We were only going from Thursday through Sunday. That was a blessing, and we were able to stay at her relative's house for free. Jurnee's grandmother was an angel sent from heaven. She seemed to always be extra nice to me. I loved her family; they always embraced me with much love.

Chapter Sixteen

Our trip was long and hot. I had never been to Tennessee or even on a long road trip. When I was ten my father took his family, his girlfriend at the time, her kids and myself to Florida, but we flew. I had never driven anywhere further than Chicago and that was just a long 2-hour ride from Milwaukee. Man, it took us about 10 hours, but we finally made it. Jackson, Tennessee looked dusty and country and the weather was like an outdoor inferno, but I liked it. All the locals were cordial and hospitable. Everybody you came in counter with smiled, *How you? Hello. Hey, how you doing?* I guess that's what they mean about that good ole' southern hospitality. Lane College was undersized and most of the campus buildings were in close range. Everything was either right next door or directly across the street, the campus was small. It had two girl's dorms and two male dorms. This was a historical black college with a lot of rules. No co-ed visits, no incense, no microwaves, and a curfew. We visited the dorms, a new remodeled building where some classes would be held, met some professors, and prospective students, like myself. They had a welcoming barbeque for the new fall students or potential students rather, 'cause it was up to us to accept or reject their acceptance.

"So how do you like it so far?" Jurnee hollered over the loud giant sized speakers in the center of the barbeque.

"It's hot as hell and too many damn rules...I don't like this."

Jurnee frowned in disappointment.

"But I need some discipline in my life and a positive direction to go in soooo... I'll be joining my girl this fall!"

"Gurl, you scared me for a minute. I didn't think you were going to give it a chance. I mean yeah... it's a lot of rules, hot weather and country folks. But, it's all what you make out of it and Modesty you're a lively person. You make fun out of a dust situation. I know you'll come down here and they'll love your city-girl ass." We both laughed and hugged. I had a good feeling about this. I some how felt like this was the best move for me - a power move.

The school gave us a list of things we needed. A dorm sized refrigerator, bedspreads, a comforter, and cleaning supplies. Basically, everything you need for a new apartment, minus furniture and any other electrical appliances. I had a lot to shop for. As soon as I got back to Milwaukee, I would collect each item, one by one. I don't know what the hell was wrong with me; I was damn close to broke. I had no idea how much money I'd had spent from the money grandma left me. My last big purchase was a living room furniture set for Tracy B, at her new house. To top that off, I paid the first month's rent and security deposit for her to move back from

California after Grandma Shirley died of Cancer. I had a negative balance *and* I owed the bank. *Fuck... how careless Motley!* I cried to myself. I was so dumb and irresponsible. I didn't even know where I would get money to go to school or buy the things I needed. I'd spent $60,000 and barely had anything to show for it except clothes, stilettos and my truck, with none left for college. I resorted to taking stuff back to the store for refunds, selling my shit and asking everybody to donate whatever money they had. I didn't know what to expect from Tennessee, I just knew I was going. Now, more than ever I wished Tojoe were around. He always seemed to have my back 110%. Now, he was fighting battles of his own. His so-called friend Trey set him up with the Feds to help shorten his own sentence. Tojoe served an undercover agent and was now facing 10 to 25 behind those bob wires. In the mean time bro wasn't gonna be helping anybody without the CO's (Correction Officer) permission. I miss you Tojoe! Keep ya' head up nigga!

Chapter Seventeen

Fat Boy, one of the 'ballas' in the city, was throwing a birthday party. He had just gotten out of jail. I fucked off with him a few times and had agreed to show my face. That was my only chance to brag to him and everybody else, about me going to college. (If you were somebody, you would be there.) I wore my light brown and cream DKNY skirt set with some light brown designer stilettos. I rounded all my girls, my sister, and some of her girls, my cousins Chanel and Erica- we were ready to get our booty shaking' started.

I'm on the dance floor, bouncing and shaking that ass to every song that came on. I didn't get much interest from Fat Boy. I figured he had too many options in the room. I thought weekly visits to him in the House of Correction would eventually pay off and earn me the first choice to being his main woman when he came home. *Sike!* Shit, my daddy wifed a jailhouse love! Fat Boy did tell me I looked good and congratulated me on my acceptance to college. That was sweet of him, but this is the same nigga that pulled me up on my undergarments not coordinating. Shit, he's the reason that all my Victoria Secret's matched. I had to give him credit for that. Ever since he told me 'real bitches do real things'... it's been mandatory. He said, "It ain't ladylike to wear underwear that don't match, ain't nothin' sexy about that."

Though he did not give me the significance I expected, I still kicked it 'cause this was my last party as Modesty the "*hot girl.*" Next time it would be Modesty the "*college girl.*"

We were in front of the mirror watching ourselves break it down and some girl tapped me on the shoulder.

"Excuse me... you Modesty, right?"

"Yeah, wuz up?"

"Wuz up? I'm Carlita. I'm the one you were arguing with over the phone about JJ."

"Oh, okay."

"I just want to know if it was drama 'cause fighting words were exchanged over the phone."

"Girl, do you see these 4" inch heels and this dress? I wouldn't dare fight you in these Jimmy Choos. Besides, I was mad and talking shit about a nigga I don't even talk to anymore. I'm here to celebrate. I'm leaving for college in a couple of weeks. I don't have time for this bullshit, unless I am forced to handle my mine. If you bring the drama, I won't back down, but other than that, it's all good."

She looked shocked at my response. She probably heard I was wild and thought I would try and fight her.

"Well it's cool. I wasn't trying to come at you wrong; I just wanted to see what was up," she answered coolly.

"A'ight then." I felt mature for going about things in a different way. Any other day I would have tried 'Tae-kwon Do' upside her head.   Next thing I know, Linda was dancing right next to me all wild and bumping me purposely.   I just walked off the dance floor and rolled my eyes.   My girls peeped the scene.   We gathered at one table and conversed.   We all knew it was gonna be drama, but the point was... who was going to be down?   I saw Jurnee trying to speak to Georgette, Linda's big sister and her cousins, but they turned up their noses.   She knew then, it wasn't a choice *but* to choose sides.   They had already partnered her with us.   Jurnee thought she could remain neutral and be the peacemaker, but it was a done deal.   Linda didn't even speak to anyone.   I guess she was still pissed at me.

   After the party, Linda and her crew was outside waiting with bats, sticks and clubs.   We all ran back to safety, but were forced to exit the building by the hood security.   It was more of us than them.   We could have mopped them ho's, but they had weapons and not to mention I was with a bunch of scared asses, including Savanna.   The final decision was for us to go head-up.   Without hesitation, Linda and I were throwing blows.   I was kicking her ass, but then she bit a plug in my thigh, close to my coochie and I lost my train of thought.   I remembered Georgette whacked me across the back with a club.   My cousin Chanel jumped in Georgette's face ready to fight, but security broke us all up.   I was spazzin'.

   "Jurnee, why the fuck none of y'all helped me?" I snapped.

"I didn't want to take sides 'cause both y'all my girls." That bitch was scared and lying through her teeth.

"What the fuck ever. That ho' didn't acknowledge you when you spoke to her. She treated you like a ghost and walked right pass yo' ass. How you explain that? Huh, Casper?"

"But, but...."

"Don't try and explain," I cut her off. "Fuck all y'all."

Savanna walked up dumbfounded. "You okay?"

Chanel smacked Savanna right upside her head and she knew not to say anything else. "Ain't none of you punk-ass ho's rolling with my cousin. Y'all can hop in her shit and ride, but can't never have her back. Motley, you hang with some weak bitches... that's why I don't fuck wit' Milwaukee hos like that." She was in Mil-town to visit and celebrate with me. Chanel had moved to Atlanta less than 5 months ago, after her and Shalonda (her dagger step-mom) couldn't stand to live under the same roof anymore. They were starting to have a little *too* much in common – they were into them girls *and each other*! Chanel started to remind her of a feminine version Aunt Jessie and Shalonda, was feeling that... in more ways than one.

"Where the fuck is Maraca and Erica?" Chanel hissed.

I overheard Maraca's friend explaining the fight amongst each other. One said, "What I look like getting in her drama and her own sister ran another way? I don't even know her like that. We ain't cool like that... fuck that." Chanel and I bounced on them chickens, leaving them to find their own way home. I don't remember who exactly rode with me to the club, but fuck 'em all. We left them behind. When I got to Tracy B's house, Maraca had already informed her about the ruckus. I don't know why, but Tracy B called the damn police. I thought they might take my ass to jail for assault and battery, the way I left scratches and bruises on that wench, and not to mention I was in a 21 and up club, and was only eighteen. So, I made a wise decision and beat them to the punch and filed a restraining order on Linda and Georgette, not because I was scared, but to clear myself from any charges. I knew every time I saw them; I would have to defend myself and it would be on record in case shit got real serious. I would have the upper hand on those bitches! Imagine that, I had "such a lady" on my plates, and I was turning in to such a got-damn brawler!

Chapter Eighteen

Two weeks left and I was moving to Tennessee only to return home on breaks – Christmas, Thanksgiving, Spring break, etc. I had a bed-in-the-bag and a telephone with an answering machine. I still had a long list of things I needed with no money. Surprisingly Dillon bought me a VCR and some other miscellaneous items. I guess that was his way to make up for the shit that went down between us. I told you, I called upon any and everybody to get up outta there. I called my Aunt Kelly, daddy' sister for help. She was so happy I was going to college; she flew in to help get the remaining things I needed. She also promised to help support me while I was away. Less than a week before my departure my truck broke down. I was so distraught I prayed:

God, tell me what you want me to do. Stay here and kill myself fighting or go and better myself? I thought you wanted me to go. I thought it was meant to be. If it is, why is everything going wrong? Please provide me a way. In your son Jesus name. Amen

I was mangled in the mind; if I had to go threw all this, I didn't want to go. My truck was broke – I was broke. My spirit and excitement... all stripped. Tracy B came to my rescue. In sincerity she spoke, "Motley, please don't give up, baby. I'll do what I can. If I have to skip this month's rent and bills, you're going to college.

You will get there. It's no good for you here. I'll sleep better if I know my baby is on her way to better things. I never went to no college and for you to have that chance and not take it, would tear me apart. Please, sweetie... You deserve this." Hearing my mom say that lifted my spirits. She had really slowed down her life style and even had a steady relationship. Those words from her made me want to really make her proud. I felt bad 'cause that lady would do just about anything to assure her children's happiness, but I often ignored that, holding onto a childhood grudge.

I hadn't talked to Jurnee or Savanna since that little incident after Fat Boy's party, with Linda and her crew. Out the blue Savanna called me all excited like I didn't have beef wit her. Why did I always have to forgive them and they never forgave me?

"Guess what? I got accepted to Lane College too. I'm attending with you." She just kept blurting shit out so fast, like she didn't want me to curse her ass out for even calling. Being the forgiving bitch that I am, I got excited with her. I was actually happy she got accepted just knowing us city girls would be discerning the dirty South together had me hyped.

"Damn, you cut it close. 'Cause we have to be down there by August 24 and its August 12 already."

"Gurl, I know its last minute, but I'm packing all my clothes and I'll get my dorm assignment when I get there. I'm sure they have

Wal-Mart, to get what I need for my room. Do you have a roommate yet, Modesty?"

"I don't know. I'll find out when I get there."

She briefly hesitated and then asked, "Wanna be roommates? That would be the shit!" Now, here I go again, begging for drama!

"Yeah. It's cool. How you getting there, Savanna?" I was hoping I could bum a ride. I needed one; this could be a win-win situation.

"My older sister's driving me. We're leaving this Friday," she said, still sounding geeked.

"Really? Can I roll, 'cause my truck needs repairing?" The whole while I'm thinking in my head, she better not say no. She at least owes me this much, since she chickened out on me two times already.

"Yeah, but don't bring a lot of stuff, 'cause I got a lot myself and both our things won't fit."

"That's cool. Well let me get the most important stuff together to take. I'll have to figure out how to get everything else later." That was reassurance to my heart; I hung up in confidence. I knew then it was meant for me to go 'cause God had provided a way. We ended our call with plans to ride out that weekend. Savanna only wanted to go so she wouldn't feel like I was doing something better than her, but I could live with that. I just knew not to expect her to hold it down with me if drama followed me down there, but hopefully I wouldn't have to.

Then here comes another call... Jurnee, pleading and apologizing to me. "Modesty, I'm sorry, I wasn't down for you. I made a bad judgment. Forgive a sista...please. Don't let it cost me our friendship. I promise next time I'm jumping regardless of the situation or the person. Shit, I am really sorry. I'd jump in and help you fight your own sister...shit, your momma. Gurl, I'm helping, I'm down for you and I'll prove it," she pleaded.

I bust out laughing. "Gurl you'd fight my momma with me? You so crazy."

"You know what I mean, Modesty."

"Gurl, I know." Even though she did me wrong, I missed our friendship; after all she was my best friend.

"What a relief. Now that, that's out of the way, you still going to Lane?" She asked sounding relieved.

"Yeah, I decided to take advantage of their offer. Savanna is going too, so I'm riding with her on Friday."

"Where's your truck?"

"Broke."

"Ugh, Savanna got accepted too? Don't you wanna ride with me?"

"Naw, I'm cool, since I already made plans to ride with her." I didn't want any mix-ups; I had a sure ride with Savanna. Jurnee didn't care too much for Savanna ever since her man tried to push up on her. Just like your typical female, taking it out on the victim, not the perpetrator. Imagine how she would have felt if she would have known Kevin use to be Tracy B's little boy toy? (A secret I'll die with.)

🕷 🕷 🕷 🕷 🕷

Right before school started I got some micro braids, until I found out who the hottest town beautician was. The first day on campus was so stimulating As soon as we got to Jackson; we registered before we moved anything in. We took a shower at a motel then headed to our new home. I pinned my micros up in a cute up do. It was hot as hell. I put on my shortest fitting blue Calvin Klein jean shorts. They molded to my ass and gave the illusion of thickness. I always had a padded bra to boost my twin cities (breast) 'cause Lord knows I had none. I felt cute and ready to catch some action. We got our final financial aid papers, took ID's, and received our room assignments.   Yep, Savanna and I officially became roommates. Why did I do this to myself?

Chapter Nineteen

The college scene was new and different for me. There were people from all over the world. Chicago, Mississippi, Florida, Detroit, Nebraska even International exchange students from Brazil, Trinidad, Jamaica and Africa with their own look and style. But one thing was for sure, you could tell the girls from up North and the boys from the South. Most of the guys from Florida had gold teeth or dreadlocks. A lot of people were already cliqued up from the campus visit when they met during orientation. Others were forced to combine because of the room arrangements. I'm glad I wasn't forced to room with a complete stranger. Before I came to LC (Lane College), Jurnee shared the horror roommate stories – Bitches stealing, snooping, lost in love, and not liking each other; crazy shit.

We 'spic and spanned' our room from top to bottom. We were some cleaning sisters - sanitizing everything. I unpacked what I had and was settled quickly. I had to go to the airport in Memphis to pick up my other boxes. Since Aunt Kelly worked for an airline, she shipped them as if they were hers. I packed everything I owned from winter coats to boots and it was nowhere near winter. Jurnee laughed hysterically at my college inexperience.

"Damn girl, you act like you ain't never going back home. You could have got winter stuff over Thanksgiving break and took your summer clothes home. You don't bring everything at once."

"Shit, I had no idea. I'm new to this." It seemed that I moved every item I owned in that small ass dorm room. I had a lot of shit, mostly boxes of clothes and shoes.

When we finally got our room organized we went to Wal-Mart and purchased food and other little things we needed. I was so excited for classes to begin. It was four of us from Milwaukee: Jurnee, Savanna, this boy named Ezel and me. Classes started on Monday and I was so ready. I picked English for my major because I liked to write short stories and poetry. It was the easiest major to graduate without too much math. I hated math – I swear if math were a person, I'd kill it!

College sure did do a body good – I learned that early on. If you got up early enough, you could catch breakfast. Shit, nobody missed lunch, and the evening wasn't complete without hittin' the café for dinner. Not to mention this is a HBCU, so you already know we had soulful cooks up in there! I had always been petite, flat chest, barely a bootie, but my legs and hips made up for that. My girls teased and called my hips, 'those child bearing hips.' I had the best legs, compliments of running track damn near all my life and wide hips, which made up for what ever else was missing which evened out my frame. The hips were compliments of good dick, I say because I couldn't tell if they were a family inheritance. Nobody had hips like mine. I was a hot commodity on campus and off. I mixed and mingled with a few locals. Most of the local females hated the 'out of town' college female occupants, contrary to most of the males, who couldn't get enough of that educated pussy. It was hard enough that this was a small hick town but then with all of these fine, young city girls temporarily filling up the city, made it even harder for these county bammas to find their mates. They didn't know me personally, but later, when I tried out for the football cheerleading team and made it. And when my ride got fixed and I drove that bitch down there, they became familiar with me. See down south they loved red bones; the lighter the better (no harm to the brown skin or chocolate girl beauties), especially the dark niggas. It was nothing like a high yellow girl to compliment their black ass. College life - so far, so good! I started to get the hang of it and I was enjoying it. I met this cute lil dark cutie from Florida, Marciano and yes - he had gold's all up in his mouth frame. He wasn't my usual balla, 'cause he dressed nice and he played football. He didn't have that tough thug persona. We got acquainted quickly, hittin' it off lovely.

We were only in school less than a month and Savanna was already acting funny. I didn't have a dorm size refrigerator, so I had to put my things in with hers. When she got in her moods, she'd act like it wasn't enough room for my things. We'd go grocery shopping and we'd have to buy two of the same things. Sometimes she didn't want to share depending on how hungry she was or what temper she was in. Shit had become so artificial between us. She was a selfish miserable bitch on campus and she kept showing me that. I wish somebody had told me ahead of time that rooming with a friend ruins the friendship 'cause that bitch was acting like an enemy – she turned sour on me. We barely even spoke. She started throwing comments about how much she hated being at Lane. She thought she was missing something at home. She wanted to be under that nigga at home, Ace; another hustling ass nigga that she started screwing. She took her pussy woes out on me. I just ignored her ass.

Most of the time Jurnee stayed in her own room. She wasn't as sociable as she was at home. She hung with two girls, Lisa and Rochelle from St. Louis. We were still close, but she had her friends and I had mine. We all got together occasionally and kicked it. Jurnee had a car and at the time, none of us did. My truck wasn't down there as yet. She often offered to drive us to a club. It was a little hole in the wall club called Hollywood, but it used to jump every Wednesday night - college night. We didn't miss a Wednesday night going there after our first visit. This was the only night Savanna looked forward to. It never failed; our routine included going to the Waffle House afterwards and getting full on the expense of Anthony, the only balla (at the time) we knew in Jackson. He was tall and handsome, wasn't too stalky or too skinny - he was just right. He dressed really nice and smelled good too, but he'd damn near fucked every girl at Lane. Just like the girls at home, girls on campus dropped panties quick when a moneymaker was involved. He was the man on campus and he wasn't even a student in college. He would pull up in his big body Benz and the chicks would flock like pigs to slop. I was even attracted to him, but knew he was off limits. He fucked with too many females I was acquainted with, including Savanna. She fell for his charm and that seductive smell of Curve Cologne along with every other female. It was a done deal after that. He fucked her once, and never called her again. Why do niggas do that shit? That shit fucks with a female mentally – it really does! It has us thinking we were the ones that did something wrong. What female wants to be labeled as just a nut? Most times you couldn't tell if men wanted you for your body 'cause they were pussy hustlers – cock hounds. Don't get me wrong, some guys might make you feel like they loved you, but most of them just wanted the booty. Shit like that left some females borderline... losing it!

🕷 🕷 🕷 🕷 🕷

College wasn't about education for everybody. I quickly found that out. Some came to escape dangerous life styles; homelessness and some came to hustle. Like this chic name Stephanie, for instance who was a sophomore but a senior whore. She used to work as a stripper on the weekends. I'd heard college tales about girls stripping to pay tuition, but no way - not this one. She stripped to maintain her expensive fetish for designer clothes and drugs. She turned tricks for money. Personally, I thought she was a nympho. She sexed freely all over campus.

Everybody had their own hustle going on at school. I even joined in on a small move with this guy named, Kwame. That saying is so true, you can take a person out the ghetto, but you can't take the ghetto outta them. That described me to the 'T'. So, you know when Kwame approached me with a scheme, I was wit' it. We were in the same Bio (Biology) class. He was one of my favorite male friends on campus. We used to keep each other up on gossip. I would tell him the latest female talk and he would tell me about all the guys. We never hooked up on the fucking tip. I found out later that he was afraid to come to me like that in fear I would shoot him down. He said, "Modesty you seem to be too high maintenance for me. I'd rather settle wit being your friend instead of try'na play myself." Honestly, I think the real reason was, he had a little 'sugar' in his tank. Dude had too much bend in his wrist and twist in his walk. Whatever his preference – he was my nig'. Anyway, we were sitting in the student center when he told me about his scheme. He wanted to open up a bank account with about eight hundred dollars. Let the money sit for about a week until the checks came in the mail. Then use the hell out of the checks, without the money to back it up. We would snatch the $800.00 deposit back, before the checks cleared on Monday. He knew the bank's routine of clearing their checks and everything. The plan was to go to the department stores, purchase merchandise and return it the next day for cash. He knew which stores had a 3-day clearing policy on checks – those were our target stores. I was diggin' his plan for us to get some cash. Our school financial aid refund checks would not to be issued for another couple of months and I was low on funds. I told him let me sleep on it and I would get back to him in class on Wednesday. I called home and went over the plan with Maraca, 'cause if anybody could pull off a scam, she was the 'it girl.' She said it sounded slick and added that we should report the checks stolen after we wrote them. When we met at class, I told Kwame let's get it crackin'. We opened the account in my name (dumb ass me), waited for the checks to come and burned any and every store in Jackson that was accepting them. We did this for an entire weekend. Kwame had done this before 'cause the stores he chose were putty in our hands. That nigga was a master at it; he could steal the crack out of your behind, and you would never know it. He knew exactly which items to purchase to later return for the cash. He paid me five hundred off top, just for getting the account in my name, plus I got stuff to keep in each store we hit. He got digital cameras, clothes, shoes, groceries and some more shit. He was a real life hustle man and I loved that shit. I knew this little city didn't have a clue what was going on. These little country hos were too slow to come up with a plan like this. I told Kwame to include me in any hustle he came up with thereafter. It's just too bad he transferred, shortly after. He was caught, ass up, with another male sweetheart, in the boy's dorm. He was outta there before breakfast the next morning when they got busted. I knew he was sweet on some dick! I guess I should say – sittin' on some dick!

Chapter Twenty

Being away in college seemed to make everybody at home miss me and view me as a different person. Some were actually proud of me, while others placed bets on how long it would be before I dropped out and came home to stay for good. Dillon used to call me at all times of the night and morning, like he desperately missed me. He called at 4am one time and this pissed Savanna off. She answered and threw the phone across to my small twin sized bed; it almost hit me in the head. I mumbled on the phone with Dillon for a few minutes, half sleep. But when I hung up – I was wide-awake to check her ass about her stank-ass attitude.

"Bitch... you almost hit me in the head."

"You know I didn't try to, but it's really irritating that he has to call at indecent times," she said in a nasal tone like she had a sinus infection.

"He's not calling for you; so you can go back to sleep instead of listening to my conversation," I countered with more animosity in my voice. Savanna must have drunk a cup of 'get-tough', 'cause I knew she wasn't trying to take it to another level.

"I wish I didn't have to wake up to that damn phone anyway at all hours of the night and morning. Some of us do have class in the morning!"

"Bitch, and I don't? You don't hear me complaining when ya ass is crying on the phone to that nigga when I'm try'na sleep!"

"Whatever, Modesty."

"Yeah, whatever to you too, Savanna." I was tired of this bitch and her bullshit. Rising up on my elbows, I stared at her and dared her to say one more thing, so I could have a reason to hammer that ass. But she didn't, 'cause she knew not to cross the line with me. The bitch talked a good game, but she knew the real... I would burn her ass faster than a New York minute. That was our first 'real' college argument. Can you believe we stopped talking for three months because of that? Once more we were on that shit – I sure could pick friends! We remained roommates, but we didn't speak at all. It was a repeat of the Cold War in our room. If the phone rang for either one of us, we would pass the phone and not utter a thing to each who was calling. With Savanna acting shitty, I started hanging tough with a girl named McKenzie from my math class. She was from Nashville aka Cashville, home of Young Buck from GGG – G-Unit! McKenzie was a little country and chunky, but cute. She was caramel toned with medium length brown hair. She spoke with a deep country accent and had one gold tooth in the front of her mouth. She was ghetto as hell, but I liked her right away. We decided to become roommates next semester. I planned to ditch Savanna's ass (for good this time).

☗ ☗ ☗ ☗ ☗

Lane's curfew was 11:00pm on weekdays and 1:00am on the weekends. If you came too late - you got in; but you had to sign your name on a sign-in sheet. If your name appeared on the list too often, a warning letter was issued to you and your parents, threatening to kick you off campus. Nobody took that shit seriously, especially on party nights.

Homecoming was approaching everybody was trying to get their gear together. I begged Maraca to send me some of her best gear. She always had the latest so; I knew she would hook me up. She was a shopaholic and was straight on the fashion tip. She never had any money, but stayed laced. All courtesy of her credit card scams and fake checks. She was the hustle woman in the flesh. 'Ms. Stay The Fuck Fly,' by any means necessary. My package from her came Friday morning. I was nervous, 'cause I didn't think it would come in time. She'd sent me a cream Polo sweater with the matching hat... a blazin' green colored Coogi jogging suit...a black fitted Versace dress and a pair of non-prescription Moschino glasses. She hooked a sista up! I would really be *'that'* bitch on campus now. They already jocked me! When they peeped my homecoming threads, I knew they were gon' be J' (jealous). To me, I could wear some bullshit and still have more style than those nonsense-ass ho's. They'd still say I was dressing my ass off. I used to wear the weakest DKNY button ups with some khaki capris and DKNY slides. That weak-ass, cornball shit turned heads. Anyway, homecoming was the shit. A lot of oldheads came back. Damn, LC was the stompin' grounds for a lot of ballas before I came and boy did I love an educated thug! Holla back niggas! I was all over the place kicking it with the fine ones. Then I had to go and get myself in a crazy situation. I was chillin' outside with Marciano on the side of the dorm in a secluded area, getting freaked. Man, this nigga I was toying with had a skillful tongue on him. I had on a skirt for easy access. He was exploring my pussy like an astronaut in space. I was backed up sexually – this nigga was right on point. We were busy right there on the stairs. And, I dare you to act like you ain't never get boned in a crazy-ass location! However, this was a place that I thought was secluded because it was closed for repairs. I was right in the middle of my explosion, when I spotted two guys and a girl trotting down the steps smokin' a blunt. I heard the squeaky sneakers and released my grip on Marciano and tried to cover up quickly. Too late – they noticed. Walking pass, they clowned my ass. I couldn't see their faces, but they definitely saw mine. The next day the incident traveled faster than the Pony Express. People were laughing and pointing. For weeks, people yelled out comments behind my back. I was so embarrassed; I wanted to transfer. Not to mention, I was a cheerleader and he was a football player. After that, I shared a bad name with Jaysa, another girl on the squad during my whore period. It was rumored (and rumors had some truth to it) that she had gotten wasted and out of control and let a couple of football players run a train on her. I don't know how true that part was, but she did admit to stripping butt-naked when she was drunk, and *claimed* to still be a virgin. People thought they left their shady past back at home, so they made up new lives when they got to college, but if the students got wind of the truth, it was sure to be all over campus. You could not hide those skeletons in your closet... somebody would expose your ass, trust!

Chapter Twenty-One

Christmas break came fast and I was excited to be home. Everybody missed me and was very curious about how college life was treating me. Christmas break was a full month. Maybe that was too long for me, Modesty the drama queen. Soon as I got home, I put my truck in the shop. I wanted to drive it back to Jackson. Maraca gave me a loaner while I was home. A two-door red Chevy Cavalier. She said it was her little hoop-tie ride.

Back on the scene, I went with what I knew... JJ. Time away from him was good. It started off innocent but after we smoked about ten blunts, my ass was ready to get into some trouble with him. We went out to eat, JJ, his friends and me. As usual, just like a pretty bitch, I got MAC lip glass all over the blunts that were passed. JJ's friends loved that shit, 'cause that was as close as they would get to real bitch. *Real bitches do real things.* I was high, horny and hungry. Yes, I hooked up with his no good ass again. That first love shit kept me coming back... maybe it was the back shots that had me addicted. *I guess*??? We snuck off to the restaurant bathroom and got a quickie in the lady's room. My adrenaline was pumping. I was trying to hold back my passionate screams so the patrons couldn't hear me. Instead of screaming like I normally did, I let out low squeals. I couldn't wait until I got him in a real bed. I was gon' really let loose. I started to think I had white liver or something 'cause I always wanted to fuck.

On the way home from the restaurant, after an evening of fun, the mofo police pulled us over and ruined my night – punk mothafuckas!

"Let the window down!... spray some air freshener... fuck!" JJ was paranoid.

"Damn, man. I'm on paper and I got this scale on me. This by itself can get a nigga time," Ronnie (one of JJ's friends) complained.

I wasn't worried. I had my lie straight and I knew I wasn't speeding.

"Bay, I got this sack of weed. Take it, you know if they run yo' name, you cool. They not gon' sweat you. If they run one of us in, we'll get cuffed on GP," JJ pleaded.

I was thinking I'm cool. I haven't been in any trouble - no tickets, no warrants. They'll let me go. I grabbed the sack and stuffed it in my panties before the two officers approached the car.

"I want everyone to step out the car and put your hands on top of the hood," the nasty, redneck officer barked.

I overheard the second officer radio for a female officer to the scene. My heart dropped. The only reason they would contact a female officer was to pat me down. The plastic bag from the weed started pinching my pussy lips, causing me to twitch. The police ran everybody's name. They let JJ go, but kept Ronnie and me. They made Ronnie do a 5-day commitment in the County jail and gave him a paraphernalia charge for the scale he had in his coat pocket. As for me, the red Chevy Cavalier Maraca *"loaned"* me as her 'little trapper' (another name for hoop-tie) was reported stolen from a used car dealer. *That bitch!* The female cop patted me down. Thankfully, she missed the weed sack. I was placed in the back of a patrol car - sick wit' it! Tears streamed down my face and my throat felt like I had swallowed a golf ball.

"Bay, don't cry. I'm coming to get you." JJ tried to comfort me. I couldn't get my thoughts together... a stolen car, weed irritating the hell out of my shit; I needed to get my ass back to school like yesterday! I was on the brink of throwing my college life all away on the strength of what?

"Call my sister JJ... 265-0874."

On the way to the county jail, I reached down the back of my pants (the female cop didn't cuff me), into my panties and tugged at my crouch, making the weed drop down. I kicked it underneath the seat, and prayed that they wouldn't find it before I got away from they asses. I had weed seeds falling down my pant leg into my shoes. Nobody noticed, which was a relief. When we got to the station, they took my shoes strings, my belt and the hair pens out of my hair. I was put in a room for 4 hours. A Private Investigator came in and questioned me about the stolen car. I knew nothing and that made him stark mad. I had no idea what was going on, but

I knew somebody was in big trouble and I knew they were trying to pin that shit on me. A white man came in. He looked at me closely and blurted out, "That's not her." Thankfully! I was put in a large room with cement benches and a toilet. It was freezing cold; those bitches had me balled up in the corner cold and thinking about how I got into this shit. I was in there so long, I'd lost track of time. They were bringing women in and out. Prostitutes, dope heads, and some more social rejects. I nodded off in hopes to get outta there soon. Where the hell was JJ or Maraca?

"Modesty Blair? Who's Modesty Blair?"

"Who wants to know and why?" I snapped in my sleep, reminiscing on my past drama with females ready to fight.

"Come on. You need to be questioned again." I was nudged out of my sleep, gaining consciousness to my surroundings.

"I was dreaming. Sorry, what time is it?"

"8:30 a.m."

"Don't I get a call?"

"Yeah, after questioning." The cold look on the officer's face gave me the chills.

"Don't I need my lawyer present or some shit?" I learned that watching Court TV.

"You have the right to remain silent until a lawyer is present. Anything you say or do can be held against you in a court of law." Shit, I didn't even have a lawyer. I laughed at myself about that one. When he finished reading me my rights the officer stated, "I'll let the investigator answer any questions you have."

I was then put into a small room with a big reflecting window. I also knew from TV it was officers on the other side, looking and listening. The investigator was tall and lanky. He had bad breathe and stained teeth like he smoked cigarettes and drank too much coffee. His attitude was shitty, matching his appearance. He threw a lot of papers on the table ordering me to sign 'Sharon Downy' about ten times. He didn't ask any questions, just collected my signatures and left. I sat for 30 minutes before I was taken into a room and told to strip naked. I felt so invaded. The female officer checked thoroughly, this time. It seemed like that dyke was getting off feeling me up. It was so degrading – rubbing and twisting; she was probing with her fingers for hidden treasures in my intimate parts. I swore that dyke was trying to make me cum. They drove me over to the female holding dorms and gave me a two-piece orange suit, some white bloomers, a pair of socks, a pair of thong flip-flops and a lunch bag with a thick ass piece of bologna with a stack of butter in the middle of hard ass bread and a carton of milk. I was placed in a real jail population with cells and a roommate. Those bastards took hours before they let me use the telephone. The first person I called was Maraca.

"Maraca, what's going on? Come get me out of here!" I cried into the phone.

"Modesty, what did you tell the police?" She sounded nervous.

"Shit, I don't know... *shit!!* I know I need to get out of here. Come and get me," I continued to cry.

"I called; you don't have a bail. You're under investigation."

"For what? Why the fuck would you let me drive a hot ass car? That's some fucked up shit, Maraca. We're blood. How you gon' do me like this? I expect shade from those other phony bitches... *but my own sister?*"

"Did you tell them who you got the car from?" she asked, ignoring my words.

"What the fuck do you think? I didn't know not to. You should have put me on?" I countered back, in a forceful voice.

"Shit, Modesty. You snitchin'? I hope you didn't mention my mothafuckin' address!"

"Bitch, you're worried about the wrong thing. I'm here - you're not! You need to make something happen."

"Soon as you get a bail, it'll get handled. Calm down."

"Has JJ called?"

"Yeah, two times. Once to tell us what happened and again to see if I heard anything."

"Call him on the three-way... 732-6222.

"Yo!" JJ answered, excited to see Maraca number.

"Hey, bay."

"Hey, Motley. You out?"

"Naw, Maraca is on the phone."

"Wuz up, Maraca?"

"Hey, J-Rock."

140

"Maraca, put the phone down," I demanded.

"Bay, I can't take this shit. I'm starving, my hair is a mess and my cellie is a dope fiend."

"Baby, you tough. You'll be out soon. Jail is not a place to be cute. Don't be mad 'cause they don't have no Gucci flip-flops in stock," he joked. "But for real, as soon as they find out how much you need, I'll give Maraca the money. I got cha, Boo. I'm standing on that." I was relieved he had my back on this bullshit I had gotten myself into.

"Maraca is on some bullshit. She won't tell me what's going on. The police said its fraud. Somebody, most likely, Maraca gave a fake cashier check for that car. They are trying to find out what I know and if I was in on it. Bay, I don't know shit. I had no idea."

"Well, you'll be out soon 'cause you're innocent, right?"

"Innocent, until proven guilty," I said confidently. He laughed, trying to make light of the situation for me. I smiled, "You gone wait on me until I get out... you gon' hold me down 'til I get back out there?" I joked with him.

"Fa' sho. I'm gonna wait for ya'." We both cracked up, knowing good and well, that soon as either one of us had an itch - it didn't matter too much who we let scratch it.

"Hey Bay, what did you do with the weed? Did you catch a charge for that?"

"Naw, I hid that shit in the back of the police car."

"Girl, you crazy?   You should be out by tonight or at least tomorrow. You'll be alright."

"I love you, JJ. The phone is about to hang up."

"Love you too, bay always," his voice trailed off.   The dial tone hummed in my ear and the thought of hearing my cellie pee and smelling her shit again made my stomach turn.   She was withdrawing off heroin.   That's the worst shit a person can witness an addict going through.   I faked a headache and was given two painkillers to put my ass to sleep all night.   Tomorrow, I was going home.

🕷 🕷 🕷 🕷 🕷

Fresh out the slammer and home to some drama.   Maraca didn't give a flying fuck about me, so I ratted on her ass. Yep... I snitched. Told everything I thought would be helpful to get my ass home.   Yeah, and?... So the fuck what – she put me out there like that! Fuck what you heard!

JJ's snake ass didn't know when to expect me home.   How else did he welcome me home? Damn sure not with open arms... instead, I caught him in the car with another ho. I had just gotten my truck out the shop, but I rammed it into his taillight so hard, it busted. I shouldn't have even played myself. He jumped out trying to be superman.   His outlook of me had changed that quickly all that 'I love you always' was straight bullshit.

"Get out the truck so I can fuck you up," he hollered trying to impress his new bitch.

"You no good ass nigga, I should kill you. I hate you!" I was so angry. The pain kept stabbing me in my heart. Why did this nigga always lead me on and why did I always fall for him? "Jump in front of the truck if you want to. I won't hesitate running right over yo' dog ass. You don't give a fuck about me. I'm in college; but you'd rather have a high school drop out. I hate you. Stay the fuck out of my life!" I cried.

"Look at what you did to my car, Motley. I'm gon' fuck you up!" I pulled off leaving JJ and that bitch in the street, fuming. "I got you faded. I got you, Motley!!"

I woke up in the next morning to the crashing sound of my truck windows. Can you believe JJ turned bitch... bitch ass nigga sure did have me faded. He had four of his little flunkies bust out my windows. These actions convinced me to take my ass back to Jackson a week early. Tracy B helped me pay the deductible of $500 toward the $1,500 bill for my windows. The insurance handled the rest. It was New Year's Eve and I was forced to spend it on the highway in tears (this was starting to be my secret pastime). My New Year's resolution was to never fuck with JJ again and to return home as less as possible. I know I said it a few times before, but I meant it this time.

🕸 🕸 🕸 🕸 🕸

When I got to Jackson my hopes of moving back on campus early were crushed by the school's policy. Unfortunately the dorms didn't open up until after the New Year. Full of Cola, and No-doze, I stormed the highway to hook up with my cousin Chanel and bring in the New Year at 112, the hottest club in the ATL. Chanel was happy to see me. We hadn't seen each other since her visit to Milwaukee when all the drama popped off with Linda and her crew. She was shocked that I murdered the highways doing 10 hours alone from Milwaukee to Jackson. Especially, not having a problem doing 6 more to ATL. We kicked it so hard catching up on the latest in each other's lives. Although we never mentioned it, the family knew of her private affairs with Shalonda when her mom went to jail, which most likely brought about her half-breed sexuality, (in lame terms - she was bi-sexual). I know my auntie was flipping over mattresses when she found out! What the fuck though? She exposed that lifestyle to her kids. Chanel was now a full time stripper, living single, sexy and her money was right. My cousin was a cutie, in fact, the cutest female in the strip club that she worked in. I learned that when I went to work with her one night. The club was called Jazzy-T's, ghetto as hell. I had intentions on dancing (go figure), but I chickened out. I even got dressed to do the damn thing. I had on a blue fitted sheer shirt and matching blue thongs with some clear see-through stilettos. I spent $30 on a waste of an outfit. Some guy gave me $20 and said he'd be right back for his dance. He said I had the perfect shape and a pretty face, but he didn't return. I figured he was drunk and forgot... oh

well.   I got most of my money back and I got
dressed vowing to never try that one again.   I
don't knock the hustle... but it's not for
everybody, especially not me.   No matter how
broke I got.   I couldn't see myself dancing for
cash. I just didn't have the heart to flaunt my ass
freely with a room full of bitches and niggas.

Chapter Twenty-Two

Second semester was better than the first. Savanna stayed home, not returning to school. I referred to it as 'super dick sick'; that Nigga she had, had her gone. That was the first nigga she had to ever really take care of her. He was the first nigga that ever gave her money. His lil' bit of money wasn't enough to keep a bitch at home though. Her dumb ass dropped out. Oh, well!

McKenzie and I were new roommates and new running partners just as we planned. My little incident on the side of the dorm with Marciano had passed and so did our part-time relationship. He hadn't returned after Christmas break. McKenzie was dating Joseph and I was dating his friend, Skylar. We fucked on the first night and became a couple the first week we met. That's some whorish shit, I know. Fuck it; it was college love with no timelines. Having a relationship in college was just something to do. I went home to Nashville with McKenzie almost every weekend. My new habit had rubbed off on McKenzie - boosting. I learned well from Maraca and some of her friends. I was paying them half for the stolen merchandise. When I ran out of money, they taught me the ropes. I caught on quick and became addicted right away. McKenzie was with the gig. We had new outfits every week for the club. It turned into such a habit we even started stealing groceries. I guess the myth about college students was true - whatever we couldn't buy, we stole. I think we took it out of proportion though. We turned into some real live boosters. We got so good at it; we could even get shoes.

🕷 🕷 🕷 🕷 🕷

Basketball season was in. I didn't try my luck at college ball, not saying I wasn't good enough, I just wasn't into it no more. Jurnee played though. She wasn't dominating the floor like she did in high school, but she still was good at it. The boys' basketball team traveled on the same bus as the girls. Jurnee had a crush on this jock named Ryan, the team's star player. He wasn't her usual type. She liked dark rugged thugs, just like me. Ryan was high yellow – not the street type. This dude had personalized plates that read '*Ryan's way.*' I always thought it was gay for males to have personalized plates, especially ones with their name on it. That was surely a 'gaydar.' One thing about Ryan, he had some sexy ass lips and a nice ass body. Jurnee and him went on one date and stopped talking shortly after because Ryan didn't defend her when one of his teammates totally disrespected her. Now Jurnee is my girl (from time to time), no doubt, and I would never do anything that would hurt her... so, me getting involved with Ryan was one thing I considered not doing. Well... not in her presence. I didn't want to hurt her, even though I kept it a secret from her. Before jumping to conclusions, calling me more names - let me explain. I ran cross-country to condition for the track season. The boy's basketball team ran the

147

same route training for the season. Ryan used to flirt all the time, but I never fed into it. When basketball season started, the way he played ball turned me on. That may sound crazy; call me a b-ball groupie, but what the fuck ever! He was sexy on the court – the way he moved and all. His facial expressions made me put aside the gay-ass personalized plate idea that I had in my head. I was curious to know how that sweaty body would feel compressed with mine. So, I pursued him. We would talk for hours on the phone and discovered we had a lot in common. We both lived in single parent homes, both of our fathers were in jail; we were both the middle child and most independent of the family. When we saw each other, we would discreetly swap looks, feels and comments. One day in the cafe, we snuck in the bathroom together and tongued it down for the first time for almost 10 minutes. His lips were soft and warm, just like they looked. I grabbed the large bulge in is pants and my pussy fluttered. I knew then - I had to have him. I needed to feel him inside of me and hoped he could beat the pussy up. I know it seems wrong 'cause my girl had dibs first, but she let him go and I had my own rules to situations like that - if I didn't fuck or my girls didn't fuck, and my home girls wanted to get at him – he was open game. There was no real attachment or commitment to Jurnee. Personally I don't think she would have cared if I had told her in the beginning. I think I made it worst 'cause I didn't tell her at all. Because of that, it put some space between us (this time it *was* my fault). Nobody knew about our private relations, except McKenzie (my roommate) and Ryan's roommate. Skylar had no idea I was fucking off in my spare time. Sometimes it seemed as though he suspected it.

"Man, why that Nigga always looking at you like that?" he would ask.

Then I'd say, "Skylar quit trippin', you just insecure. Damn, you ain't the only one who thinks I'm pretty. You should be happy you got what another nigga admire."

"You probably like that fuckin' nigga. You think you slick." He would outright accuse me.

"Grow up. You acting immature. I'm yours, all yours. A nigga can look, but only my baby can touch." I stroked his ego.

"I better be the only one who can touch, let me find out another nigga stroking my pussy!"

I hated when Skylar got in his insecure moments. It made me feel paranoid 'cause inside I knew I was being dirty. Ryan wasn't even all that cute. Shit, to some he was ugly, but he scratched my itch when I needed him too.

One night while Skylar was at a football meeting, I met Ryan at the park. We played on the playground of ecstasy that night. We fucked from the merry-go-round to the slide, to the bench and finished in his back seat. His dick was long and thick and I endured every inch of that pipe. The nigga could' a been gay – you know they say gay men have real big thangs! He hit it hard from the back with me bent over holding the bench for support. I enjoyed it more while he stood over me on the slide with my legs almost to my head. My back was throbbing from the pressure of the slide pressed against it, but the pleasure of his motions made me ignore it. He sent me to multiple climax heaven that night. I gave him the explosion of a lifetime when I straddled his ass in the back seat, riding him like I was in the Kentucky Derby, jocking for the 1st prize.

"Damn, Modesty. You got a wet shot."

"You like it?"

"Hell yeah, I like it... work that back!"

"How much? Tell me how much," I moaned.

"Yeah girl, ... you know you making it feel good. You working that pussy...yeah, baby. What you trying to do to me, get a nigga sprung?"

I had that nigga whimpering like a begging puppy, until we both froze to a blinding light in our faces. Dayum! Busted! The police caught us right in the act. Windows all fogged up, sex funk in the air. I think the cop was more embarrassed catching us, than we were being caught. He took our names, address, telephone numbers and scared us a little and then released us with warnings. The only reason he let us pass was because he said he was a LC graduate and knew the pressures of the no co-ed visit rules. But, he also warned us not let it happen again. We got a motel room every creep after that!

Chapter Twenty-Three

Just when I thought I left all the bullshit and hating ass ho's in Milwaukee, I ran into one just like 'em in college, except she was from Bolivar, a small, almost nonexistent little hick town outside of Jackson. This bitch was cornbread country. I don't see how she wound up in college. She looked and acted like she belonged in the cornfields. No offense to all the ugly, country ghetto broads, 'cause education doesn't discriminate, but this ho' was rude, obnoxious, country, ugly, and wild. Plus, the goblin loved nose candy (cocaine). She was ruthless, fat and sloppy. Anyway, her name was Kenya. She had been bumping me, mugging me and watching me – all the things a bitch would do when they don't like you. But the problem was - I didn't know why. Shit, I didn't even know her. I mean, I seen her face around campus. Saw her in the club a few times, but when did that make us enemies? I got that mystery solved on Skylar's birthday. He rented a suite at the Micro-tel Hotel and Suites. His guys were all up there chillin' and I stopped by to have a couple of drinks and to tell him I'd be back later with his real gift. I had planned to wait until he left the room for the club and come back and decorate the hotel room with rose petals and candles. When he returned, he would find me covered with whip cream around my titties and pussy with chocolate swirled around my body. I

Precioustymes Entertainment

gave him a hint when he asked what I got him for his birthday. I told him save room for dessert. I boosted him a Sean John shirt with a matching cap. I gave nice gifts, even though they were stolen. (He didn't know that though.) Anyway, Skylar was walking me out and we stopped at the soda machine. He stood behind me, hugging me over my shoulder when a girl's voice shouted, "What the fuck you think you're doing?" We turned around and it's this freak, Kenya. Skylar told me to ignore her because the bitch was crazy. Kenya started screaming to the top of her lungs. "*Crazy!* Was I crazy when you was hittin' this pussy, like this was yo' last piece of ass?"

"What's going on? Is there something I need to be on familiar terms with, Skylar?" I asked sarcastically.

"Yeah, tell her Skylar. We've been fuckin' since y'all ain't together... right, Skylar?"

"Shut up, bitch. You mad 'cause I won't fuck wit' chu'. You just hatin'."

"Naw, nigga I ain't 'cha bitch. That's ya' bitch right there. I ain't gotta hate. I have you more than ya' ho do." Skylar charged her so fast. He slapped her and was holding her by the neck. "Ho, I'll kill you. Don't come around here disrespecting my girl. I'll kill you." He was vexed.

The front desk clerk was shouting, "Security, security. I'm calling the police." Roland, one of Skylar's friends grabbed Skylar off of Kenya.

"Come on, Sky. Man, she ain't worth it. Fuck her man; don't get locked up on your birthday." Skylar let go of his kung fu grip and spit on Kenya. Some of Skylar's other friends Dewy, Zoë and Vernon laughed hysterically. I just stood there in shock.

Kenya looked at me, "What the fuck you looking at? He's only fronting in front of you. He'll have his face in this pussy again by the end of the week." Skylar jumped at her like he was going to hit her and Kenya ran like her ass was on fire. Roland had to calm down the frightened clerk. He told her it was a misunderstanding and it was settled. It was no need to call the police. She obliged and threatened to put them out of the hotel if they caused any more commotion.

"Come on Motley, I know you didn't let that trashy ho' get to you." Skylar held my face in his hands.

"What?... you fucking trash now, Skylar?" I pulled my face away.

"Naw, I can explain." His friends were snickering in the background.

"Come on. Where's your truck, so we can talk privately." We sat in my truck and my emotions let loose. I cried for the first time in front of Skylar. I thought I left this drama at home. I came here drama free, enemy free; now look at what he got me into. Kenya was calling me out my name. She'd been fucking with me, though I ignored her. I didn't know the whole time she was fucking my man.

"What's next, Skylar? Am I going to have to fight over you?"

"Naw, Baby. Don't cry. It's not like that. You haven't got shit to worry about. I got 'chu, boo... I got 'chu. I'm gon' handle it. I'm gon' fix this, I promise. I love you, girl. I'm not gone let nothin' happen to you." This mothafucka was sounding just like JJ's tired ass. I wasn't buying what he was selling.

"Skylar, tell me what that was about. Please tell me the truth. I'm not mad. I just want to know the truth."

"Okay, this is how it went. When we got into it one night at the club, I was pissed at you and got drunk. I heard you were fucking that basketball nigga and Kenya was watching me. She saw me exchange words wit' the nigga. When I left the club, she followed me outside. She came right up on me and grabbed my dick boldly and was like, *I bet I can make you happy. I won't make you mad.* First I pushed her back, but then she started talking real nasty. She's all like; *I've been wanted to suck your dick since I saw you on the schoolyard. I want to fuck. Is you game?* Shit, Motley... that shit sounded real good in my ears and my dick was getting brick hard. I was so mad at you and drunk, I fucked her. Everyday after that she started stalking me, buying me shit. Talking 'bout I couldn't leave her alone that easily. Man, that ho' is crazy." Skylar lowered his head. "Baby, I'm sorry, I fucked up. I'm not trying to put you in a situation like in your past. Come on, Motley... give me another chance."

I sniffed, "Skylar, did you fuck her this morning in that room?"

"Hell no. I'm not gon' lie though... she paid for it. She was mad 'cause I didn't give her a key. I told her the room was for us."

"Well, we're getting another room at a different hotel after the club, so you get your stuff together." I fell for some more bullshit. Jackass must have been written on my forehead.

"Okay, Motley. Whatever you want, Baby. It's cool wit' me. I'll see you at the club. Wipe your face off. Don't ever let anyone see you cry in public. They'll think you're weak. I love you, girl."

"I love you, too," I answered, still in search of unconditional love.

Skylar and I took pictures all night at the club and danced on every slow song, with Kenya watching in anger. Every time I looked her way, she rolled her eyes. I just laughed.

🕸 🕸 🕸 🕸 🕸

A week later, I let Skylar use my truck and I rolled with McKenzie, in her Honda. When we pulled up on the schoolyard, I saw Skylar and Joseph in my truck and that monkey-ass slut Kenya was standing at the driver's side conversing with Skylar. I jumped out the car before it even stopped rolling. Kenya walked into the dorm as I approached.

"Give me my keys, Skylar!"

"What... you mad?"

"Why you got the bitch all at my shit, disrespecting my ride, talking to that ho' in my shit? Just give me my keys."

"You don't even know what I was saying. I was checking her for you." I knew his lying ass was trying to convince me with his weak ass game. I grabbed my keys and walked away. Skylar came behind me. "You gon' walk away like that?" He grabbed my arm. I snatched away and kept walking. That must have touched his nerve, 'cause then he yoked me by the neck and started cursing me out.

"I'm checking this ho' for you and you get mad at me! Acting like a little bratty bitch!" The dorm mother came out. She was a nosey old lady. "Let that girl go - talking to her like that." I tried to play if off. I kept a smile on my face, pretending like everything was fine.

"I'm okay, Ms. Wilma. We were just playing."

"It don't look like he's playing to me and it don't sound like it either."

Skylar grabbed me in a bear hug and smiled. "We fine, Ms. Wilma. You know this my Boo. I'm just playin' with her."

"Yeah, okay." Ms. Wilma sneered and walked back inside, looking over her shoulders. She knew we were lying.

I hopped in my truck and pulled off furiously; getting played was becoming a bad habit of mines. I could see that smirk on Kenya's face when she walked off. I bet she was laughing at me. I just know that trick better not had been in my ride. I didn't talk to Skylar the rest of the day or night.

The next day after class, Skylar was waiting in front of the dorm.

"Hey, Baby." He gave a tight squeeze before I could get "hi" out of my mouth. "Before you snap, here." He handed me a motel key.

"Is this compliments of ya' girl again?" I said smartly.

"Naw gurl, this one's on me. Meet me there at 7:00, so we can talk." He walked off before I could agree. But I knew as well as he did, I would be there.

McKenzie and I hit the mall like we usually did after class, on our boring days. We had almost every Baby Phat outfit Gold Smiths and Dillard's sold, that we could steal. We might as well have been official Baby Phat models. On the way back to the dorm, we ran into Kenya and two of her hood friends. They kept driving the same pace as me, trying to keep up. I parked in the back lot of the school to a secluded area, where Kenya had a chance to start some shit. As soon as I got out, she charged me up.

"What's up, Modesty? Laugh now," she threatened me. "I heard you was dissin' me. Why you tell Sky I be bumpin' and mean muggin' you?"

"Look girl, I don't even know your name. Skylar told me you were on some shit 'cause he don't fuck wit' you," I said, not backing down.

"He's a damn lie. He fuck wit' me every time I want him to. He said the only reason he won't leave you alone right away is because he needs your truck. And, he say he don't want to be bothered with your cryin' ass!"

"What!" I had to say something to kill her ass 'cause she was damn sure killing me with words. "Well, that's funny since he told me, you are a crazy, trick ho' and a coke head."

"Where he at? We can confront the nigga together," she countered.

"I don't know. But, if you run into him before I do, tell him I said I'm through fuckin' with him." I was lying. Later, I'd be at the Motel with Skylar to confront him alone. Fuck her! It was about me; I left her there and walked towards the dorm. I spotted Roland and Dewy hanging out.

"Y'all remember that crazy bitch that came to the room trippin' on Sky's birthday? She just came at me in the parking lot. What's up wit' her?" Dewy just shook his head. Roland was the first to open his mouth to give me some type of answer. "Sky gon' fuck her up. If I were you, I wouldn't even worry about her. She a clique ho'. All of us hit that," he laughed. That made me feel a little better, but I needed me some Sky to work my stress out. Everytime drama came at me, it seemed like I had to get a nut off. I went inside the dorm and packed my overnight bag. McKenzie packed one 'cause she was going to stay at Joseph's, in the bricks. The bricks were the projects down the street from the school everybody lived in for about $25 a month – lucky bitches! I dropped her off and headed for the motel to meet my baby. When I pulled into the motel parking lot, I noticed Kenya and her hood friends following me again. This time, Roland and

Dewy was in pursuit along with them. At first I started to keep driving, but I knew they would only follow me, so I parked. I hesitated to get out at first. I wished I still had my 'hater-beater' stick in the back of my car from home. I had no other choice but to get out and face whatever was about to happen. Immediately Kenya rushed me.

"You called me a bitch to Roland and Dewy! You were questioning' them about me?" She pushed my head. Roland began to laugh. I got in stance. I already knew it was time to throw down. She swung on me and we went at it. Dewy tried to break us up, but Roland was rooting on the fight.

"Let 'em fight," that grimy ass nigga egged.

I felt like I was in a good position. I wasn't really winning, but I wasn't losing either. We fell to the ground. That's when Dewy broke it up. She was holding three of my micro braids in her hand. She cursed at my back as I ran up the stairs to get Skylar. I banged on the door hysterically.

"What's wrong? What happened?" He asked startled. He was with one of his friends, playing Play station. I couldn't get my words out fast enough. Panting for breath, I told him, "Roland let Kenya fight me. He followed me here with her and we just fought. They still outside." Skylar ran outside. I grabbed a beer bottle off the table and ran out behind him. When I got outside Roland and Skylar was all in each other's face arguing.

"Nigga, how you gon' do my wife like that?" Skylar was heated.

"I didn't know Kenya was going to follow her. She was taking me to get something to eat," he fired back.

"Whatever! That nigga is lying, he wouldn't let Dewy break it up!" I screamed.

Skylar charged for Kenya. She ran and jumped her car and locked the doors. Dewy pulled Roland into their car and they all pulled off. I examined myself in the mirror for bruises. Thankfully there was none. However, I did have a big ass bald spot on the side of my head; a clean spot like hair never grew there from her tight grip on my shit. I was able to hide that with other braids, so no one could tell.

Word got around the school fast. People were coming up to me, left and right. *"Modesty, I heard you had a fight." "I heard you got dog walked by Kenya." "I heard you were fighting over Skylar."*

Every question I was like, 'it must be a mistake; that wasn't me.' They all thought either I was crazy, or Kenya lied. I didn't have a problem with her after that. She was probably still fucking Skylar, but I never heard anything else about I and I didn't ask. Fuck it; he was only my temporary college love. Wasn't no future in him. A nigga gone be a nigga, anyway! I just knew not to take the mothafucka serious from this point on.

Chapter Twenty-Four

Valentine's Day was approaching and I had no idea what to get Skylar. He got outfits from me so often that it wouldn't be a surprise. I wanted to get a good gift. I had started to think of JJ lately; dreaming about the good times we shared. I wouldn't dare fuck back with him. I knew he was toxic for my health, damn near fatal, but I did call him to wish him a Happy Valentine's Day. This was our first Valentine's Day apart in four years. Wasn't anything wrong with calling to say "hi" and to catch up on what was good in the hood! I was pleased that his number was the same. As soon as I heard his voice say hello, I fell in love all over again.

"Happy Valentine's Day, stranger," I said cheerfully.

"Who dis?" JJ quizzed.

"Who you want it to be?" I cheesed, hoping he'd recognize my voice and not disappoint me by saying another bitch's name.

"I want it to be my baby, Motley, but she hates me. So, I don't know who this is," he joked.

"Save it nigga... good game, wrong person."

"Hey, baby. Happy Valentine's Day to you, too! I didn't think you would ever talk to me again."

"You know me... Ms. Unpredictable. N-E way, how you been?"

"I'm cool. Got a little cold, but I'm maintaining... and you?"

"I'm cool, just doing the school thang."

"Who you doing the school thang wit'?" JJ laughed.

"What kind of question is that? Am I questioning you?"

"Get out yo' feelings. You know your boy been around here?"

"Who?"

"Dillon."

"For what, and with who?"

"Him and Lil boy hanging kinda tough, ever since your shindigs you used to throw."

"Funny, really funny. I see you're a real entertainer."

"Yeah, I know - I miss you, too."

"Who said I missed you?" I had to hold some ground.

"I knew you wasn't gonna let our first Valentine apart go without a word."

"Oh, you noticed. How many valentines do you have lined up?" I asked sarcastically.

"Just one," he laughed 'cause he heard me gasp, "and that's the only woman who truly loves me."

He killed my mood. "Okay then, have a nice life JJ. I'll call you around your birthday, if you're not married."

"Look at you... still hot headed Motley. I was talking about my daughter. She bought me a card and some balloons."

"You mean her mama bought," I corrected him.

"Yeah, but the words say 'for daddy', so it's from her. I'm not even gonna ask how many gifts you got 'cause you always havin' your way with men."

"I wish... well I was just calling to say Happy Valentine's. Holla."

"Dag, short and sweet. You gon' call before my birthday?"

"Yeah."

"Alright, baby."

I wanted so badly to hold a long conversation with JJ and tell him how much I missed and loved him, but the nigga was a serious heart disease. I didn't want to fuck around and get dick sick like Savanna and take my ass home. No way, I had to get off that phone.

"Bye, JJ. Stay out of trouble."

"Anything for you, Motley." Then there was silence. "I love you, girl."

"I... love you too, JJ." He still had that power over me. I was glad that I was in Tennessee, if I'd have been home, I'd be on my way to his house. I also thought about calling Dillon, but I was still upset from when he drove to Mississippi and refused to travel three more hours to Jackson to see me. How I regret not calling, 'cause Happy Valentine's Day would have been the last words we said to each other, instead of '*fuck you.*' Later I found out, Dillon was found shot in the head two times; he died instantly. No funeral either...he was hood orphan. Come to find out, he was 3 years younger than me, but the hard-knock life made him look much older. For the second time in my life, I mourned. The nigga was bad news but he was still an 'alright' dude. I felt bad that he had to go out like that.

Chapter Twenty-Five

Summer break rolled in real quick. Instead of being smart and staying three extra weeks in Jackson for summer school like Jurnee, I rushed home like a fool. I don't know why 'cause I also rushed for the end of summer to come, so I could haul my ass back to school. There was a rumor circulating that I supposedly had something to do with Dillon's death or knew something about it. Everyone thought JJ and his little brother set that up 'cause Dillon was last seen alive at a gamble held at their house. Since I was the one who connected them and everyone knew JJ was my ex, they made their own speculations. But what the fuck ever, like I'm some kind of 'Gangsta Boo,' setting shit up all the way from Tennessee. I don't think so. Even though I had both of them on restriction, I wouldn't want to see either of them hurt.

◆ ◆ ◆ ◆ ◆

I was relieved when Aunt Lauren announced her road trip from Milwaukee to Atlanta. She wanted me to help her drive. I agreed to go, only if we could stop in Tennessee. This trip was just what the doctor ordered. I drove the entire way, even through the rainstorm. I was excited 'cause Skylar was still in Jackson for football training. When we finally arrived in Tennessee, we got a room to shower and change clothes. Aunt Lauren agreed to drop me off with Skylar so she could go spend some time with her husband, Edmond, better known as ED. He was locked up in a prison just outside of Jackson. He committed a crime in Milwaukee, but was shipped to Tennessee due to overcrowding at the state jails. They had been a couple since the age of 14, and got married at 21. He proposed to Lauren after he was caught cheating again for the umpteenth time. He didn't know how else to get her back but to prove he loved her by marrying her. Aunt Lauren agreed feeling like that would be her revenge on all the women who ran behind him. Now at age 32, he had been in jail 7 years of their marriage. She wasn't all that faithful, but she stuck in his corner damn near the entire bid, playing her role as his wife. She traveled ten hours almost every other weekend after that, only to sit for 8 hours on Saturday and Sunday visiting her man. Not I, there was no way I was spending my break from Milwaukee in anybody's jailhouse visitation area.

As soon as I got out the shower I called Skylar to find out his location. I had to go watch the kids in the pool until my Aunt was ready. I swear I would rather have a dog then a kid; at least you can put dogs in a cage without being charged for child abuse. Aunt Lauren had two girls, Lasha and Alize. Black folks know they some fools when it comes to naming their kids. Aunt Lauren said Alize got her name because she was full of it the night she was conceived.

Lasha had on a float, but Alize didn't. I guess she thought she could doggy paddle the short distance from the wall to her sister's float.

They were in the middle of the pool, right where it sinks down to the deep end, sinking, screaming and panicking. I felt like *Super Woman* the way I ran and dove into the pool. I grabbed the one without the float. I damn near had to pry them apart. Both of them were holding on for dear life. I think I scared the hell out of them. They cried worst because of the way I yelled at them, rather than being relieved that no one drowned. The aftermath was hilarious. For some reason, all of the children feared my authority. I was stern and straight up with them, like my daddy was with me. What I said goes - no questions. They were pretty much terrified, that they upset me. Most of the kids in my family listened to me more than their own mother's. I believed in street discipline. If it wasn't one thing I hated, it was an unruly, smart mouth, badass kid. Don't get me wrong - they were bad and grown, but when I was around, they kept that shit to a minimum. I don't think they hated me. In fact, I know they admired me. Most of my little cousins did because they thought I had it all - no kids, dressed nice, kept a fly nigga and talked like I knew everything. They loved that shit.

Lauren ran to the door when she heard all the uproar. I came bursting in the room, soaking wet and furious, with the kids not far behind, coughing and crying at the same time. Lasha ran to her mother's embrace. Alize shot in the bathroom and shut the door. Skylar was waiting on me, but now I had to re-shower and re-dress, not to mention re-do my hair. I had my hair cut really low with the textured look. My hair curled up real cute when it was wet, but I had to mold the front so it would lay just right. Lasha apologized until her tear ducts ran dry. I had to buy her a Popsicle to prove to her I really didn't hate her because of the way I hollered at them.

When everybody was dressed, we were on our way. They dropped me off in the bricks with Skylar and continued their journey to the correctional facility.

Chapter Twenty-Six

There is a good ole' saying that calls the beginning of a good thing, the honeymoon stage. Shit, they ain't lying. The first two days with Skylar was like cold water to a hot thirsty throat – it felt good. We laid up almost all day. I enjoyed the morning breath and nerve gas that we shared. I watched TV or slept in when he had to go to football practice. Things were all good... until curiosity set in. I was wondering why he got so touchy when I reached to answer the phone. So, when he left for practice the next time, I wasn't ignoring the phone – I was answering it! Now I see why people say, when you go looking for bad things, bad things you will find. If I could go back to that exact day, that exact moment, believe me you; I wouldn't have been so damn nosey. Every time it rang, it was, *"Skylar there?" "Where Sky at?" "Who dis?" "Where is Sky-Boogie?"* Nothing but, easy access cock calling! Ho's I knew from school, including the bitch I had already fought, Kenya. I shared my secrets with this nigga and he was still pillow talking with these guttersnipes about me. I couldn't wait till he came back from practice, so I could blow up his spot. Soon as he walked his funky ass through the door, I went off. I was out of breath trying to rank on his ass.

"Nigga, you fucking ho's... talking shit about me to these ho's; telling them you don't fuck wit' me! You nasty, lying, gritty dick ass..."

WHACK!! He smacked the shit out of me before I could get 'nigga' out my mouth. I was petrified. Normally I would strike in frenzy, but Skylar had this bizarre, wickedness in his eyes that made him.

"You shouldn'a answered the damn phone... catering to these scally wags, telling them shit we do behind closed doors... shit we talk about. Telling them how a nigga be eatin' yo' pussy and shit. What the fuck is wrong with you? You can't come up here trying to run a nigga, especially when you at home fucking and sucking any dick that has money acquainted with it. Them hos knew you were coming this weekend. For those who didn't, I put 'em on hold. You just had to go answering the phone and starting shit. Got bitches up to my practice telling me all this shit you said."

I was crying and holding my face. I watched my tone 'cause I did not want him to pimp slap me again. Even I knew better than to try a nigga who was mad. "So you came home ready to attack me, 'cause of what some ho' ran and told you at practice without clarifying it with me first???"

"Did you clarify anything before I stepped halfway in the door and you snapped out. Hell no! Damn... you couldn't even let a nigga wash his sweaty balls first."

My feelings were mostly hurt because he was still talking with the same goblin I had drama with - my enemy. I know I said I didn't give a fuck... but I did! We argued all night, until he fell asleep with his back to me.

A day went pass with no words exchanged, on the second day Skylar packed a small duffle and told me he was going to Memphis for the duration of my stay. I asked him if that included me. He frowned at me like he smelled something dead.

"Naw, you straight. I really don't want to be bothered with your troublesome ass any more. Can't you tell? A nigga ain't much as touch you or held a convo with you in a day and a half?"

"Damn, Skylar. That's malicious. I drove all the way here for you and you leaving me here alone, hurting."

Skylar had a hostile glare in his eyes; staring at me as to say, *I don't give a fuck.* "You were coming this way anyway; not just for me."

"What the fuck else was I coming for? My people had other plans; you were my plan. They way in Atlanta and they're not coming back this way for another two days. What am I suppose to do until then?"

"Shit, play on the phone like you've been, since you been here. What type a 'fuck nigga' you think I am?" He turned his back, slammed the door and left my ass sitting there sobbing to a dirty ass room and dirty stained walls that had no heart or remorse, just like him. The first thing I did was call Chanel's house, collect, and tell them what just happened. And just like I knew she would, Chanel demanded revenge.

"Seek vengeance, then leave."

"Where am I supposed to go? I don't have no ride and not enough money to last in a room for two days."

"Don't you have some friends somewhere around? Where's McKenzie?"

"We fell out in the beginning of the summer when she came to Milwaukee... a huge misunderstanding."

"If she's your girl, she'll squash that shit and come get you."

"Naw, I did her dirty. She probably hates me. I haven't heard from her since."

"Damn, that's deep. What happened?"

"Don't care to talk about it right now."

"What's her number? I'll call for you."

"Okay, but if she acting shady, don't kiss her ass...(615) 259-3383."

We hang up and 10 minutes later, Chanel called back.

"McKenzie will be there in an hour and a half, so be looking out."

"Damn, just like that?"

"Yup, she was happy I called. I told her small details and she said she's on her way with no hesitation."

"Damn, she still my girl. Thanks Chanel, I gotta get my shit together so I can bounce. I'll call you when I get wit' McKenzie."

"A'ight, but don't leave without leaving your mark. And another thing Motley, if you stop being so vindictive, it wouldn't come back on you. Ya' feel me?"

"I heard you." I hesitated. "What should I do?'

"I dun no, but make sure he feel it; make him wish he wouldn't have fucked with, Motley 'G' baby!

"I thought you just said to stop doing foul shit to people."

"Naw, I meant to your immediate circle. Fuck a nigga! Do him in somethin' terrible." That got me gassed up. I had all type of thoughts racing through my head, extreme shit to do, to leave my presence. After 30 minutes of packing and contemplating. I gathered all Skylar's remaining clothes, shoes and what everything else he owned in a garbage bag. I poured beer, ashes, bleach and soup in the bag and shot it in the large garbage dumpster in back of the projects and set them on fire. Then right before I heard McKenzie's horn, I wrote, *'You will feel my pain'* on the kitchen floor with a permanent black marker.

Soon as I got in the car, I apologized to McKenzie for making her first trip to Milwaukee terrible. She brushed it off and smiled. "Wanna go shopping?"

"Hell yeah." I knew exactly what that meant. Booster's open season!! We hit up our favorite stores, just like we did during the school year. She had her handy dandy censor remover right on deck. We shared it, passed under the fitting room doors. We called it the 'popper', as a code name and called sensor tags 'crybabies', and we had no trouble popping those crybabies right off. I had mastered the field of boosting by now. We did this for two days straight; until Aunt Lauren was headed back my way to return to the placed I called home. I came back with way more stuff then I came with. You might as well say I went school shopping, since school was 5 weeks away.

Chapter Twenty-Seven

Sophomore year came and went as fast as it started, but not fast enough to get rid of the dark clouds that seemed to always rain on my parade. McKenzie and I were back tight without anybody at school ever knowing that we fell out. I hadn't run into Skylar yet, but I was prepared for when I did. We hadn't talked the reminder of the summer from the drama that occurred during my visit. He called once or twice, but I never returned his calls. I finally bumped into him in the café on the 3rd day of school. He acted like he did not see me. I walked up on him while he emptied his tray of food.

"Hey, Sky!" I acted like everything was peachy and creamy.

"Ohh... hey," he replied dryly and walked off. I followed behind him.

"Show ya' girl some love. Don't you miss me?" Skylar looked at me like I was shit on his shoe and replied with disgust in his voice, "Did you show me love when you burned all of my clothes? You think I'm some soft ass nigga? Am I supposed to forgive you? You got me fucked up. I'm not fucking wit' yo' scandalous ass no more. I got a new bitch and it's not Modesty."

I have to admit I wasn't surprised, but I was salty 'cause if it's one thing I hated – it was that bitch – rejection! I had to find out who his new girl was; I needed to see my rival.

Over the next few days, I heard rumors Skylar was messing with Jaysa, the phony scank from Detroit that I used to cheer with on the squad.   Out of all the females he could have chosen, it had to be her.   She always made me feel like she wanted to be me.   I knew that cunt was a snake. We were on the cheerleading team together and shared mutual associates, but there was always a chill in the air between us.   She was one of the haters that used to say dumb shit.

"Modesty thinks she's the shit.   The only reason she dresses like that is 'cause she steals." She used to make small comments to me like, "Can I get it how you get it?"

Of course I never fed into it 'cause that would make my guiltiness obvious. I used to tell the broad, *"Get it how you live."* It had been many times and many situations where I should have beat the brakes off that ho', but I didn't.   Now, I wish I would have just on 'GP.' This bitch was fucking with what I still had claims on - Skylar. If that wasn't bad enough, out of nowhere McKenzie announced she was transferring, not just to another school - but also to another state. My girl was leaving, packing it up and going to Florida Memorial in Miami, Florida.   She never really gave me a real explanation.   She was running from something or somebody. I couldn't figure it out but I knew it had something to do with Joseph. She was gone before the thought of her leaving, settled. I was disappointed, but I had problems of my own to worry about. That was one strange thing about myself I couldn't figure out. No matter how attached I was to girlfriends, it was easy to settle for *'out of sight out of mind'*.

         N N N N N

The semester went by quickly. Skylar and Jaysa was the new hot item on the campus and it was butchering me. Although I had my flings, I did not get heavily involved with anybody else. The shit had me sick wit' it. I lost my appetite, my enthusiasm, and my sparkle. Nothing else mattered to me anymore. I wanted my man back - or, just away from Jaysa. Everybody knew they were a couple and it scoffed my insides every time I saw them together. I wanted to fight her so bad, but I knew that would make me look stupid. When I did see them, I kept my composure, trying to leave my ghetto-ness at home. I had to concentrate on my studies; apply myself to my education.

Chapter Twenty-Eight

Homecoming had come so fast, I almost forgot to get right. As usual our football team lost the homecoming game, but Skylar shined the way he always did. He was the leading scorer. Later that night, at the club it was my turn to shine. I made sure I saved my best outfit for the step show on Saturday night. I wore my tightest fitting Versace pants. They were purple, green, black and yellow and yes – the logo broadcasted the fact that they were designer. My shirt was fitted with the same colors and it showed my supple round nipples. And to put the icing on the cake, I wore my glass stiletto sandals. I was a showstopper – finest thang walking… *"Gorgeous."* I decided that if I didn't get my man back tonight, I was going to charge it as a lost. I didn't have to work hard 'cause as soon as Skylar and his crew entered the club I was the first thing he saw. I was standing in the picture area, posted up with my girls, taking major snaps. I had sex appeal written all over me. Skylar immediately made his way into my view. I flirted with my body and then invited him into our own personal photo shot. We posed for more pictures. We posed holding our middle finger in the camera, meaning, 'fuck the world.' He held my ass on some poses and even posed with his face by my pussy, claiming it as his. Of course, someone signaled Jaysa to witness this for herself. She watched in fury.

I whispered in between snaps to him, "There's your girl."

"My girl right here. You're who I want. Fuck that skeezer." Niggas always fell for my crazy ass – if only for a hot minute! I think they loved the crazy bitch that was inside of me! That made me smile, and show off even more 'cause I knew she was looking. I almost cashed out (spent all my money), trying to keep this private show going but then I had to remember the night was young and I wasn't buzzing yet. As soon as we finished, Jaysa rushed Skylar.

"What the fuck, Sky?... with all this disrespect."

"Yo', you see me with my girl. What up with your disrespect?" She looked foolish and I looked like a winner. Her friends pulled her off, sneering at Skylar. In all reality I should have dissed his ass for all the heartache and misery he put me through, throughout the semester. But me being the average girl and weak for him, I fed into it all. I was happy to have my man back. It all seemed like a sham, but just like he quit fuckin' with me - he was back fuckin' with me.

"We back, boo?" I had to make sure that the bitch was cancelled.

"Fa' sho, shorty." I gleamed, knowing now she was disposed.

"You mine, right?" Skylar questioned, not sure if I had another man yet.

"Yeah, you mine too, nigga. Ride or die."

"Always was, I just had to teach yo' as not to treat me like no 'fuck' nigga. I never liked that plastic ass ho. She was on my dick. All she wanted to talk about was you, and I knew I could use her to get under your skin.

"Wit' cho' dog ass," I smacked his arm.

We were back a hot item, 'the couple' of campus like nothing ever happened. Now Jaysa was sick wit' it... and I had my swagger back. God really knew what he was doing when he created man. It was weird how the touch of a man could give you the feeling of security, his voice gave you assurance and his words gave you promises, but at the same time the men you loved the most, inflicted the majority of your pain. Skylar and I completed the year like we were never interrupted. Life was good for me and I had no complaints at this time. What a change!!

❍ ❍ ❍ ❍ ❍

I went home for Christmas break to find Maraca had been arrested for that car shit, along with the rest of her scams, exposing her criminal activity. She had already been on probation for credit card fraud and forging signatures, so she had to serve out the rest of her probation time, which was one year and she was, facing a new charge. I knew she had to be busted and disgusted. As soon as I touched down in the city, I went to visit her. Although some of my past statements affected her freedom, she was my blood and I still had her back regardless of her devious ways.   As usual, Tracy B cared for Mariah.   My mom now lived in a nice quiet neighborhood with her fiancé Wallie (and not a young joint), Austin and Mariah.

I missed my sister not being at home. I was use to kicking it with her, lacing me with all type of things and looking out for me. However, for the time being, that was dried up. The saddest part was seeing her in jail and Mariah crying for her on a regular. The thing that broke my heart the most was when I took Mariah to the mall and she desperately wanted to see Santa. I was rushing and did not have time. I told her I would take her at a later time. She began to whimper. Her eyes swollen with tears, she said, "I just wanted to tell him to bring my mommy home for Christmas. I don't want no toys; and I been a good girl." The pain shot right to my heart. I felt helpless for my little boo, and I felt horrible for putting my sister out there like that. She knew I gave her name up and wasn't even mad at me. With her being in jail, I should have learned a lesson to stop boosting, but me being 'Ms. Rebel... Ms. Hard Head', I had to learn on my own.

🕷 🕷 🕷 🕷 🕷

It was a big party being thrown for the Milwaukee Bucks Basketball Team and I had to be there, dressed to impress. I hooked up with Savanna (who was back at home chillin' with her nigga) and I went to the mall ready to shop our style for the party. I had stepped up my boosting game and thought I was untouchable in any store. I already had in my mind what I wanted to bust, so I knew exactly what store to hit up. I wanted to rock a black leather mini skirt with a waist high black leather coat, with stiletto thigh high boots. We went straight to Wilson's Leather factory inside the mall. I picked my selections, worked the store and headed for the dressing room. I was now a master of my craft. It was easy as stealing candy from a baby. I did my thing and I was out. I walked through the mall waiting for Savanna to call so we could meet at her car. One hour had passed and no Savanna. *Ring! Ring!*... It was a number I didn't recognize on my cellie. I was hesitant at first, but I answered anyway. It was Savanna; she was calling from the back room of the leather factory. This dumb bitch went and got herself caught. And the fucked up thing about it was - she had only stolen a pair of leather gloves and a leather cell phone case. She was what I considered a miscellaneous thief. I, on the other hand, had a $500.00 leather coat with the matching mini skirt. As soon as I answered, I heard her crybaby ass voice.

"Modesty, you gotta come back. They won't let me go, unless you bring back their stuff."

"What? Who is this and what are you talking about?" *That snitch ass bitch!* Shit definitely comes back to you!

"Come on, Modesty. Don't play. They already know."

"Know what?"

"Seriously, they know who you are and what you have."

Right then my heart dropped to my feet and it felt like I had swallowed without chewing. I hung up, and before my phone-timer stopped blinking, my cell was ringing again. This time it wasn't Savanna; it was the police. Savanna had run it down to them - my full name, address and telephone number. The snitch even gave my mother's maiden name. I felt like I didn't have any other choice. I wasn't gonna run for this small time shit, when I had gotten away with thousand of dollars worth of stuff at other times, from major stores – Bloomingdales, Neiman Marcus, Abercrombie & Fitch, Banana Republic, BEBE, and more. Now, here I am with this petty ass ho', at this petty ass store and I get nailed for the first time. And on top of all of that, it was the weekend and Christmas was less than 5 days away. Now most people wouldn't have gone back. But I did, only on one condition - I was not about to risk being brought through the mall in handcuffs and being the talk of the city on some thieving shit. I told them I would meet them in the parking lot by the furthest entrance with the merchandise. I picked an entrance in the back of the mall, a not so popular entrance anybody hardly used. I already knew I was about to be arrested, so I prepared. I couldn't get in the car 'cause the snitch bitch had the keys. I got rid of other stolen items I had lifted from other stores. I threw a lot of things away. I didn't give a fuck 'cause I didn't know exactly what they knew. I kept the skirt, pretending that was all I had. When they approached me, I was automatically searched and handcuffed, put in the back of a police car and driven to the nearest police district. Savanna was already there. We were put in separate rooms to keep us from conversing. It seemed like forever and a day. Cops kept coming in and out with too many questions. Then the last cop came in and busted me.

"There's a coat missing from the Leather Factory and your friend said you have it. We didn't recover that from you, which means, one of you is lying. Neither one of you are leaving this place until it comes up."

All I could think of was to stomp the shit out of Savanna when we were finally let lose. After one hour of stubbornness and denial, I agreed to take them to the coat. When I did, they gave me a fat ass ticket and a court date. The only reason I didn't go to the county jail is for cooperating and I agreed to pay for the skirt on spot. That allowed my theft amount to be lowered. It was now a misdemeanor and not a felony theft. I guess it could have been worst - like the weekend at the county jail eating baloney sandwiches with butter in the middle and swapping dessert for juice with dope fiends.

We got a free ride in back of the police car back to Savanna's car. The first thing she said when we got alone was they had us on tape. I wanted to hit her so bad, but we were in her car and far from my house. I wasn't about to catch the bus; that cramped my style. It was too damn cold and I didn't feel like explaining to someone else why I needed a ride. Heated, I rode home with Ms. Walkie-Talkie in complete silence. My mind was thinking all type of vindictive shit - mostly cruel revenge. She got off light though. All I did was bop her one good time the minute we got in front of my house. I was not only mad at her, but at myself, for not learning from Maraca's situation.

Chapter Twenty-Nine

To almost everyone's surprise, I was one year away from graduating from college. Me, 'Modesty Yameyeia Blair'. The one everyone doubted and labeled as an, 'undeniable ho,' and an 'unambiguous failure.' I was only 18 credits hours, plus 4 electives away from graduation. That meant the rest of the year and one more semester. Although, I still had one year to go. I had proved at least 80% of the statistics wrong. That's a hell of a percentage. It wasn't time to boast and brag yet, but I had a reason to celebrate. I had counseled with my advisor, Dr. Hodges to complete my schedule for the next two semesters. I had my major classes scheduled, Sociology, Intro to Social Work, The Exceptional Child, etc. I wasn't feeling the writing style, so I ditched English as my major. My shit was straight up ghetto Literature 101: uncut. I wrote real shit...street tales - not no Shakespeare, Harry Potter type fables. They wanted suburban kid material. Fuck a 20-page paper on bullshit topics. The Stiletto Queen only wrote true to life shit!

❖ ❖ ❖ ❖ ❖

Things seemed calm for me, which was unusual seeing as how I'm usually *"that bitch, always with the drama."* Skylar was drafted to the NFL. He was a 2nd round pick for the Denver Broncos. All that fucking finally paid off! I felt lucky that I was wifey – his wifey especially! I was so glad we got back together. That meant becoming an NFL wife with access to all the doe. With Sky going to the NFL it brought lots of Media attention to little ole' LC. It wasn't until I read the article on Skylar that I knew about his big plans. In the article that asked a few questions about his personal life, they asked him whom he was going to take that big move with. It sure wasn't Modesty Blair. My fucking luck! Skylar mentioned his son back in his hometown and his son's mother, Nicole. He told the press that they were high school sweethearts and planned to be married in a year. If I had never been made a fool out of a day in my life, this certainly put the icing on the cake. Everybody read the article and of course me being the most hated, they ate off that shit. Jaysa had a ball off out of it. Her and the 'gym shoe' crew loved the fact they had something to hold over my head. But that's not what bothered me the most; it was how I kept letting men play me. Before I could even get at Sky, he was outta there – gone, just like that! He already knew he couldn't handle the pressure that I was gonna bring. After that major blow to the stomach Sky gave me, I was fed up with college dick, so I chilled on finding temporary college love. Ever since that humiliation, I basically became a campus tease fuckin' with niggas, but holding out on the ass for a change... but only for an educated moment. I walked around in my belly tops tight jeans and everything else, strutting my new seductive shape. I had gained a few pounds in the right places since my matriculation at

Lane. Other chicks hated, because they couldn't control their college pounds.

◆ ◆ ◆ ◆ ◆

My tease for the semester was Gary. No, I didn't miss a got-damn beat! He was 25, no kids, had his own crib and a nice ride. I attracted him in particular because we had the same truck, different colors. I met him at the carwash he happened to own. His pick up line was corny, "nice truck." He started off comparing our trucks, which eventually led right to, "Can I get those digits?" I got a free car wash, and we started to hang out tough. That was before I found out my new roommate, Corrine, had a short affair with him the semester before. Corrine is cute, butterscotch dimple faced, with a deep southern accent from Mississippi that many called, 'bones.' She was mixed with rich African and Cuban blood. But if you let her tell it, she was Irish, Puerto Rican, Indian and whatever other nationality you could be mixed together. It depended on what holiday it was – she celebrated them all! Every holiday she gave praise to herself, celebrating her nationality. She was tall and slinky with dark brown mid length hair that fell just below the dimples in her cheeks. She was what most guys considered sexy, if you liked that runway model look. She was all right with me and had actually hand picked me to be her roommate for the semester. It is a known fact that most pretty girls like to be acquainted with other pretty girls, and in this matter, I think this was the case. We had been casual friends since we both came to college. We both knew of each other and spoke every time we saw each other. We decided - why not be roommates? The only thing I didn't like about her - she had pretty much kicked it with every nigga worth dipping and dabbing with, on and off campus, but then I had too, I couldn't front on her. Every person name I mentioned with slight interest, she would say, "been there, done that." And of course her stories always had them begging and pleading to remain in her company, leaving her to have to break their heart by telling them her charity with them was over.

Gary called the room one day and Corrine answered the phone. I saw the salt stinging her eyes. Immediately after I hung up the phone with him, she had a million and one stories on what he did for her, how he did it, how often and so on. I left her with a blank understanding of what was going on with him and simply said, "We're just friends. We hang out occasionally and get throwed (high). That's about it." I had to make a memo to myself to stop telling the next female all of my business and missing out on something or someone that was good for me. I had noticed she did this with most of the guys she may have only had as little as a casual conversation with. If a guy looked at her, her version would be 'he wants me'. So from that observation of her, I knew how to handle with Ms. Corrine. Personally, I started to consider her a 'friendemy.' That's what I call a friend and an enemy in one. She could be a friend to a certain extent - shopping, gossiping, minor secrets; but a enemy in another - always competing for best outfit, wants to beat you at everything each of you do. We ended up having a class together - Probability and Statistics. She used to do her homework and when I asked to see it, she pretended like she didn't know what she was doing. "I don't think it's right," would be her favorite excuse, or " Gurl, I just wrote anything." She knew it was right 'cause she was hella smart... a damn math major.

✗ ✗ ✗ ✗ ✗

I maintained single status as promised to myself and drama had missed me this semester. My number was up on the rent assistance list and I was due to move off campus any month now. I had a part time job at Shoe Smart, a cheap shoe store across the street from the mall and I was getting paid weekly. I held onto this job for a decent amount of time. One evening while I helped another employee close the store, a well-dressed black man entered the store seeking church shoes for his daughter. He was unsure of her shoe size, but gave her age and wanted me to estimate about what size shoe she wore. He stated she was 6 years old, so I estimated about a size 12 in kids. If they did not fit he, could always return them with the receipt. He followed me back to the kid's section of dress shoes and immediately pulled a gun out of his jacket pocket and pointed at me. He whispered, *"This is a robbery. If you scream, I will spray yo' ass."* I think I was more in shock than scared. I did as he said by walking over to the register and giving him the money. He must have done this before, because he insisted I give him all the money out of the safe, which was hidden under the counter of the register. The other woman working with me approached; saw the gun and immediately panicked. He ordered her to shut up, stand and watch. We cooperated; I wasn't about to lose my life over some plastic shoes, purses and a couple of hundred dollars. He got what he wanted and he ran off. We called the police right away, but he got away. I learned that night that our security camera was a fake. I ended up staying with the company for lack of another job. As an appreciation I was given less than a bullshit .30-cent raise and a lousy free dinner for putting my life on the line for these cheap mothafuckas... uh, huh, not no more!

Chapter Thirty

The fall semester was almost over and Christmas break near. During my vacation home, one of my cousins got me addicted to eBay, an online auction that sold everything in the alphabet A-Z. Of course, I searched out all the designers. I had bid on and won a nice Gucci Logo spring coat. The catch with eBay was getting it when you see it, 'cause it wouldn't be available within the next hour. I desperately wanted this jacket. I imagined the fame I would get wearing it on my back. I didn't get paid for another four days because the pay period had just visited me and it was only Monday. I listened to the little voices in my head and I lifted $200.00 dollars out Shoe Smarts' safe with hopes to return it by Friday, payday - before the store manager came for the weekly drop to the bank. I got the money and ordered the jacket to satisfy my retail addiction. To my surprise, the cameras in the store may have been fake, but the secret cameras inside of the safe were real or so they said. Either way, I got caught; $200 dollars was deducted from my paycheck and I was fired with no room to explain. But, how could I explain being a black female addicted to retail? I guess only Kanye West understands that. I accepted it for what it was. I looked good in my logo Gucci jacket though. I knew it was a shame and I was too embarrassed to admit to people that I was fired for stealing money for my material fetish. So, I lied and told everybody I quit 'cause they kept getting robbed. I made it seem like my life was too important to die over some cheap shoes. Everybody sided with me on that. The only thing, I had regrets about losing my job so suddenly is I didn't have money to pay first month rent and security on a new apartment off campus. The rent assistance office had sent my letter, granting me the option to look for a new residence. My voucher was for $305, which meant I would receive double - $610 to move-in. I had to get my hustle on, so I could get some extra shit for my apartment when we returned from Christmas break. I knew off top it wasn't going to be that mini mansion I always longed for.

Instead of going straight home for the break, I ended up going to the home of my newfound buddy, Danyeil, in Memphis for a week. Danyeil was born and raised in Memphis, but from the looks of it and the way she acted, (dressed and talked) you would of thought she was your original city girl, from Chicago or Detroit. She could have even passed for a Milwaukeean. She was medium height, with a brown sugar complexion and long, pretty, dark brown hair. She said she was mixed with Creole. She was pretty... and girlfriend knew it. It didn't matter that she pledged APG (All Pretty Girls) Sorority Inc. they were known as the pretty girls on the campus; also known as conceited, stuck up and Boushie Sorority, Inc. Those that didn't know her: hated her. Those who knew her, loved her, but could get annoyed with her really fast. She had this squeaky, high pitch voice and whined when she talked. We were on the same cheerleading team during football season, but I didn't fool with her like that. Although, we got super cool when she started dating this guy from Milwaukee, who also went to college with us. Ahmad was an attractive guy. He was tall, had refined caramel skin and his hair was almost as long as Danyeil's. He kept it neat with fresh cornrows to the back. He was a keeper. I was surprised that I didn't know him back at home. He probably was a lame and found his spotlight in college, like most did. Danyeil and Ahmad had been dating almost two years. Two years full of drama, but they made it and both decided to take a year off, move together in Memphis, work full time and save some money. They planned to get married the following year. We stayed at her moms' house while Danyeil and I searched to find a new home for her and her husband to-be. She had agreed to return to Jackson with me to return the favor. Ahmad went home to work over the holiday so they could have their rent and security when they found their love nest. Danyeil had planned to hustle her 'cake daddies' to get money for their furniture. She used her looks to get exactly what she wanted and it worked perfectly. She loved Ahmad and was willing to give up all of her tricks, ballers and boy toys to be with him.

"*Main,* I can't believe I'm doing this. Modesty, you think I'm doing the right thing?" She snapped me out of my daydream.

I was dazing out the window thinking of ways to get money and where I was going to fill out a new job application. "I don't know, Danyeil. I always say whatever makes you happy. I mean if it doesn't work out, it's not the end of the world. Just learn from your mistakes."

"Modesty, you're right, but that would be fucked up. My family is really disappointed in me. They think I'm letting him change me and I won't return to school, but I'll show them. All I can do is prove them wrong."

"Danyeil should live for Danyeil. Whatever works for you, sweetie. 'Cause in the end; it's you that has to deal with the consequences of your decisions. You need to just do you and just make the best out of it and whatever won't kill you - will make you stronger." We both looked at each other with a serious face, until she busted out laughing to break the silence.

"Damn, girl. You deep. That was the truth. That's why I enjoy being around your crazy ass."

"So what are we going to do in Memphis, *main*?" I used an accent like hers. They talked a different terminology in Memphis. It was strange and funny, but I loved it.

🕷 🕷 🕷 🕷 🕷

I was excited to go home with Danyeil, because I knew she knew all the happening spots, all the real niggas and who was who, amongst Memphis finest. It was only an hour ride, but great for sightseeing. We stopped at one of their biggest malls, The Wolfchase Mall. It introduced itself and confirmed the obvious - we had officially entered Memphis. I swear every city I went to had better malls than Milwaukee. *This mall was huge!* It had a large carousel in the food court. It looked like the carousel at Great America. They had all the good stores - Gold Smith, Dillard's, the Coach Store, BeBe, Nine West, Express. They even had a Cole Haan shoe outlet. I had my popper with me, but held back from using it because I wasn't on that level with her yet. I was ready to pop every censor off of every item I had my eye on. I told myself I was going to return and hit they ass up as soon as I got a chance. We entered Express, Danyeil shopped and I played dress up, desperately wanting to go to work. She asked me if I had something to wear to the club, because if not I better find something while we were at the mall 'cause "Denim and Diamond Nightclub" was definitely the spot on Fridays. She seemed to pick up everything that was pink and green, cute or ugly. Those were the colors of her sorority. She finally decided on a pink fitted sweater with a green and pink belt. She said she already had the pants to match at home and some boots. When we got to the register, I noticed I only seen her pay for the sweater and not the belt. I was thinking, *I know this girl ain't put that belt back. I just know she did not creep it.* I wanted to know bad 'cause if she was creeping - then let the games begin! I couldn't wait until we got out that store 'cause I sure was going to ask... with no shame in my game. We hadn't even reached the exit door to the mall before I asked.

"Gurl, why you didn't get that belt? It made the outfit."

"Who said I didn't?"

"Hell naw... you creeped it?" I acted surprised, as if I hadn't stole a thing in my life.

"Gurl, I gotta do what I gotta do. Please don't tell anybody I steal. They would love to hold it against me."

"Gurl, please. If it makes you feel any better, I don't just steal – I boost." We both laughed, until our stomachs hurt.

"What's the difference?" she questioned. I had to educate her country thinking on the hustle. "When you steal, you're getting what you want to satisfy you. When you boost, you get things other people want, to sell it for paper."

"Damn, gurl. I told you, you was deep," she smiled. "So you sell your stuff?"

"Sometimes, if I need money." She looked surprised. "How do you get those censors off?" I pulled out my favorite tool, a small screwdriver with the head like a hammer, but smaller.

"*Oh shit! Heeey...*"she high five'd me. "Tell me how to use it and where I can get one from... you done started somethin' now." We headed our asses straight to the hardware store. This was the first secret we shared. From that day on we were inseparable. I drove to Memphis damn near every weekend after that.

🕷 🕷 🕷 🕷 🕷

Danyeil ended up finding a one-bedroom condo in one of the nicest neighborhoods in Memphis. With my luck, I found a one-bed room apartment in one of the dirtiest parts of Jackson. My financial aid refund check came right on time. They mailed it home and I had Tracy B, express mail it to me. I paid my first month rent and security. Once I got my apartment keys, I decided on going back home to Milwaukee for the remaining two weeks of the break. It was exciting to know I had my own place. I wanted to spend time with my family, but I was also anxious to get back to Jackson to settle in. My mom gave me dishes, pots and some silverware. Maraca had finished her one year bid and was given a hefty 5-year probation for her other charges. She still managed to help after I did her in. She bought me an air mattress and some towels. She even gave me some food stamps to grocery shop when I returned back to Jackson. I felt like shit that I'd ratted on her and she kept showing me genuine sisterly love. That stolen car shit was a mere mistake. I know she didn't intend on me getting caught out there driving it. Mariah was sad 'cause she thought this meant I was never coming back home. I had to explain to her I was just moving off of campus. She had gotten so big. She was no longer a little chubby toddler. She was a slim and slinky, 4 year old. Austin had grown into his pea head and was now a handsome teenager. He was short for his age, but kept up enough trouble. His size was hardly noticeable when the lion he held inside came out. He kept a steady flow of company. He even had little girls coming on the frequent. I felt that Tracy B should have stepped up and slowed down his role, but she said she was letting him be a man. Her comments led me right to my Aunt Lauren's to stay with her and my two little cousins. She was still on that old shit, I thought she had really changed. Or, was it just different raising boys?

Aunt Lauren was still trying to hold it down alone because ED was still in jail. She faithfully made bi-weekly trips to Tennessee, in hopes to keep the fire burning. Our family relationship had developed over the years. She was 30 something, but looked extremely young for her age. Young enough to hang out with me! When I chilled over her crib, she had me out every night I was there to the Hip-Hop clubs, Grown Sexy Night, Sport Bar's and all that. I think auntie was living her youth out through me. I heard women go through some serious trauma when they turn 30. Most of Aunt Lauren's early years were dealing with a man that kept her on lockdown. She didn't go to college; hell, she didn't even graduate high school. Too wrapped up with Uncle ED. Shit was fucked up for her. I didn't feel responsible for her newfound hobby – club hopping. It wasn't my fault she was reliving her teen years 'cause she missed out. It was that nigga, ED's fault and her own - for allowing him to steal her freedom. She was like a new woman; breathing air she didn't know existed. She was meeting people, fucking 'em, sucking em' and some mo' shit. And, Uncle ED blamed it all on

me.   One day he called collect and I answered.
He called himself roasting me, but he must have
forgot - he was the one in jail and I could hang up
and not except his calls. This one day he called, I
could tell he was upset with me because Aunt
Lauren hadn't received any of his calls this week.

"What up, Uncle ED?" I said coolly.

"You tell me,' hot commodity'. I mean
Modesty," he said with venom.

"Why you say it like that like?"

"You know why! You got my wife hanging
out in the streets missing my calls and shit.
She's a married woman, Motley. You should
respect that."

Right away I snapped, "Look nigga, I don't
have no control over what she do and how she
doin' it." I had a straight up attitude now.

"You introducing her to all these different
niggas, double dating and shit. Lasha told me
how you invited some young niggas over for you
and my wife. Just because you like to whore,
don't try to turn my wife in that direction." He
was shouting at the top of is lungs by now.

I was hot. "Fuck this, I don't have nothing
to do with who ya' wife is fuckin'. Take that up
with her. Like you said, she's a grown woman. I
didn't have to put a gun up to her head. So nigga,
fuck you!"

"Modesty, run that bullshit on somebody
else. Half the niggas I'm locked up with already
told me that you hold the title for *Miss Fuck A Lot.*"

When he said that, it really got under my
skin. I didn't care if it hurt his feeling or not.

"Nigga, go kick rocks in the jail yard... better yet, go get ya' dick sucked by one of the jailhouse homos. Let some steam off, 'cause you fuckin' with the wrong chick. You and those dick riding ass niggas, keep my name out of ya' mouths before I have a real nigga, stick his dick in it! Oh yeah nigga...don't drop the soap." *Click*.

He called back ten times before he realized I wasn't accepting. As soon as Lauren came home I told her the entire story. She scolded Lasha for running her mouth. She avoided ED's calls until she could figure out what to tell him. She told me after I went back to college; he wrote her damn near a book about me. All I could say was "*Join the 'I hate Modesty Club.' It has free admission.*

Chapter Thirty-One

On the ride back to Tennessee, Ahmad and I mostly listened to music; making small talk. We split the drive half and half. He drove the first 5 hours and I drove the last 4. He was cooler than I thought; I had never held a real conversation with him. He mostly talked about Danyeil. How much he loved her, how good she was to him and how he planned on spending the rest of his life with her. He said he was surprised how friendly she'd become, since she barely took to females. Especially, those outside of her sorority. He let me in on a big secret. He told me that Danyeil planned to come back to campus in February to make sure I was coming to the APG Sorority Inc. Rush and she was going to see to it I got in. This made me happy because I discreetly wanted to be apart of this sorority, but had never shown interest. I knew what type of doors it would open, being apart of something so productive. Even I knew this type of affiliation made a difference on resumes - especially in the community and as a reference on job applications. He made me promise not to tell her I expected her intent, and said to act surprised if the subject ever came up. I was ecstatic because I eagerly wanted to become a member. I just didn't know how I would come up with the $700 dollars it took to join. I had spent my last bit of money to purchase a $150 rug for my apartment. It didn't match a damn thing, but I planned to build my décor around it.

My apartment was small and very ugly on the outside. It wasn't as bad in the inside. I heard the building used to be a hotel. It did resemble a hotel come to think about it. It had a large living room, with a small walk-in kitchen, the tiniest bathroom and a medium size bedroom. I didn't complain because it was mine. Anything beat living on campus, sharing a large community bathroom with trifling girls you didn't know. Ho's had crabs jumpin' from toilet seats and shit. Some girls were so filthy, they used to leave bloody pads and tampons lying around the stalls or do stuff like, leave stank-ass shit floating in the toilet. I didn't know if they thought this type of behavior was funny or they were just that damn nasty. I was glad to have my own space; mine all mine.

♥ ♥ ♥ ♥ ♥

Since school started Monday and New Years Eve's was Saturday, I spent the remainder of the weekend in Memphis with Danyeil and Ahmad at their new condo. I don't know what that girl did, but their house was damn near furnished. All she needed was her living room set. Talk about somebody with expensive taste, her bedroom set alone was $4,000. She financed it, putting down $1,500, as the initial payment. Her bed sheets were 100% Egyptian cotton. Her bathroom set was 'grown-up' for real. There was no way I could compete with that. I was going to try, but I had to know her hustle. Maybe then, I could catch up.

"Girl, what the fuck? You robbed a bank, ain't it? This junk is fire!" 'Ain't it', 'junks', and 'fire' were some parts of Memphis slang I adopted. "You doing some serious flodgin' (stuntin') up in this piece."

"Gurl, you know how I do's it... Big time to the day I die... If you gon' do it, might as well do it big."

"You make it sound so easy. How can I be down? Danyeil tell me your secret, what... you swallowing now?" I said implying she was gargling semen.

"Naw, baby girl. It's called financing, with a little bit of trick money to finish it off."

"Gurl, I know you did not tell those tricks where you and ya man, gonna lay y'all head?" I asked in amazement.

"Naw, shawty. They gave me the money because they think I'm moving somewhere by myself. But now they don't know I'm fixin' to cut their water short. I holla at 'dem niggas lata."

"Damn, Danyeil. Where you meet these simps'? I'm in desperate need of a trick right about now. I need so much shit for my spot."

"You'll meet one tonight 'cause the Memphis b-ball team is having a party at the Premiere nightclub." I couldn't wait to get to the club. I got a fitted Azzure belly sweater with the matching fitted sweater skirt from Gold Smith. I already had some cute ass stiletto boots from Kenneth Cole. I had to exchange $200 worth of stolen merchandise to get them. I already had a denim and blue Christian Dior purse. You couldn't tell me I wasn't going to be marvelous. The outfit complimented my hippy ass and accented my flat stomach. Danyeil got a pair of fitted blue jean pants from Express that scrunched up on the side and a mink vest she stole out of Dilliards.

❖ ❖ ❖ ❖ ❖

The club was flooded with bodies, to bring the New Year in. There were NBA players all over the place. Memphis had just got their own NBA team and they played Los Angeles the following night, so half of LA's team was even there. Talk about 'baller heaven'. All the local celebs, ghetto superstars and all the wanna-be's were there. I went to Danyeil's hair stylist and got my butters done. I got a body wrap done with perfection by the Dominicans. Danyeil had pretty hair and only allowed the Dominicans to work up her mane. Her hair always appeared shiny and healthy. My hair had the illusion of this same texture of hair, if only for the weekend. I only got my hair done; Danyeil on the other hand, got the entire spa treatment and I admired that. She was definitely a high maintenance chick. I too, wanted to live like a hustler's wife. If this was how she was livin'. It was only a temporary thought though. All hustlers' wives paid dearly for holding that title! Everybody knew Danyeil, every turn we took, people were greeting her. She was considered one of the Ghetto's elite. She reminded me of myself when I was back at home.

Everybody knew me, I was loved by most and hated by many and so was she. She moved with such precision and grace. She had style and appeared very classy, but could go from stiletto to ghetto in one shower, like myself. This made me respect her even more. We kicked it all night. All of our drinks were sponsored from different guys she knew. We were standing around observing the atmosphere; talking and laughing at the bums who thought they had it, but didn't. They were not on our level. This crazy looking guy came over trying to spit game.

"Excuse me... Miss," he said looking in my direction.

"*Excuse you...*" I replied with disgust written all over my face. He ignored my attitude and continued, "My boy, Ron Taylor wants to holla at you."

"Why didn't Ron Taylor come approach me himself? And, why did you tell me his full name?" I was curious.

"You don't know Ron T, from the Memphis basketball team?" His smirk read, '*yeah right*'. So I gave him an, '*I don't give a fuck look*', right back.

"Well tell Ron T to come holla at me if he wants to chat."

When he walked away Danyeil, shot off right away all excited. "Gu-u-rl, you caught one! Ron T wants to holla at you. He's a million dollar nigga. He just got traded from somewhere else to play for Memphis. *Main,* he could make you apart of the Mile High club."

"The Mile *what* club?" She didn't answer because Ron T was coming up behind me.

"Hey, sexy." I seductively turned around slow and replied, "Hey you."

"Shawty, you're fine ass hell and your body is banging. Do you work out?"

"Naw, I use to run track, but cut the small talk. What up with you?"

"You... I'm trying to get to know you. What's your name?"

"Modesty," I said simply.

"Modesty what?"

"You want my last name?" He shook his head yes.

"Blair, but why do you ask?"

"Don't mind me; I just like to know a person's full name. You want to dance?"

We danced off of at least five songs, slow and fast. The rhythm in our bodies grooved as we coupled into each other's curve. He smelled so good; I had to say something. A nigga with sweet smelling cologne made a bitch putty!

"What are you wearing? It smells so good?"

"Old Spice." I frowned and thought to myself, *'Damn! That cheap shit smell good and why is this million-dollar nigga wearing a Pharmacy special?'* He must have sensed my disappointment 'cause he bust out laughing. "Shawty, I'm joking. I got on Issey Miyake for men. I wish I would wear some Old Spice."

After working up a quick thirst, we retired and he invited me into VIP. I told him I had to go find my girl first and I would meet him back there. I caught up with Danyeil and we walked to lounge with them. Before approaching the V.I.P area she enlightened me, "Modesty gurl, you caught a big fish. When I say Mile High club, I mean he's going to introduce to Chanel, Fendi and Prada as well. If you're lucky, maybe you can meet CLK," she said, smiling at the thought of it.

"Who is that? You know you have a way with words and terms girl." She had this mischievous bad girl look on her face.

"Gurl get wit' it, CLK is a sports coupe Benz. My cousin Lissy was dating a NBA player and he put her in the Mile High club, bought the bitch a CLK 430 Benz and put the bitch in a million dollar crib."

I knew I had to work it 'cause I wanted desperately to be in the Mile High Club. I imagined the envious stares of Jaysa and the rest of the 'gym shoe' crew when I rolled through campus in my Benz. Ron T interrupted my sweet daydream.

"Hey, shawty... what's taking so long? You coming to VIP or what?"

"Oh, yeah. Come on Danyeil; we in." She followed me as we walked through the crowd and everybody standing around VIP begging to get in, watched us walk straight through. It was then I knew I belonged in VIP. I was VIP bonafied and all my ho'in finally paid off. I wanted to remain at this status at all times. We drank Moet with various NBA players. One of LA's star players pointed to me and told me to come to him. Ron T saw him and waved his hand to let him know I was taken. I wanted so badly to run to his big ass. At least I knew who he was, but Danyeil said I was cool with having caught Ron T, so I remained satisfied with my catch. He was trying to put her down with one of his teammates. We stood there small talking. I couldn't wait to call home and tell Maraca I kicked it with LA's finest.

For the rest of the night Ron T kept me close to him. We talked and laughed until the night was over. LA's star player and Danyeil didn't have a connection, so they left it in VIP. Ron T and I exchanged numbers and I told him I would call him the next day. He tried to get me to come over that night, but I declined. I wanted to give him something to look forward to. At least try to save the pussy for one night.

♥ ♥ ♥ ♥ ♥

My star-studded weekend came to an end. I wished it could have lasted longer. It was back to reality in Jackson. Now it was time to get to project 'fix a house'. I wanted to make my little ghetto shack as comfortable as possible. The first thing I bought was blinds. I found some cheap wall pictures at Family Dollar that matched my rug. Yeah, it was a real project chick purchase. Next, I went to Wal-Mart and bought my bathroom set and a black entertainment center for my living room. I changed the price on it; the original price was $150. I peeled a tag from a computer desk for $39.00 and pasted the scan bar on the entertainment center and it worked. Slowly but surely, I got it together. I purchased a cheap kitchen table from Big Lots. It was a tall bar table with two matching bar stools. It was a perfect fit. I finished off my shopping with a nice café rug with the matching oven mitts and towels from Target. Tarshe': as my Aunt Kelly would call it (to make Target sound more expensive). Last on the list was furniture and a bedroom set. I decided to finance my bedroom set for $50.00 dollars a month and bought a used couch for $150.00. My apartment was complete and ready to be broke in, but I damn sure didn't wanna break it in with a NBA player. Not in this low income shit and I was try'na pop high class!

Chapter Thirty-Two

Savanna decided to return back to school after she realized her and Ace didn't have a future. He had two babies on her within the last year by two different women. The fact he had fell off, and his ballin' game was shut down, also helped her haul her ass back to school. That, with realizing the only way to advance, was to further her education. She moved right back on campus with her lazy, spoiled ass. She qualified for an apartment outside of the campus, but declined the option. She said that it was too much work for her. Me...I was trying to get my 'grown-woman' on. I was more independent than she was. And just like the others, she was jealous of me too. Let her tell it, I thought everybody was envious of me, *and did*! But seriously, I thought she was. Either that or she was on something personal. For starters, she barely complimented me when I knew a tribute was due. Not to sound cocky, but if the compliment fits, then wear it. She didn't ask to visit my house, not once. She avoided me as much as possible for no apparent reason. Our friendship was fine, last time I checked. When I was around her, I felt the negative vibes, including the resentful remarks she would make. For example I was telling her about this outfit I got from Memphis and I told her I thought I was the bomb when I wore it. Her response was, *"Don't you always"*, while rolling her eyes. Now I know a 'hater' remark when I hear one. I didn't give a flying fuck 'cause I know misery loves company and I was too happy to let her sour spurts get me down. She made me feel like she was my friend when it was convenient for her. I don't know what she was on, but I wasn't about to try and figure her out.

♥ ♥ ♥ ♥ ♥

Ron Taylor and I had become familiar with each other. We talked over the phone on a regular basis. He finally invited me to a game. He gave me two tickets and of course, I took Danyeil. We had some good seats, almost directly behind the team. Ron T barely played, but I still I enjoyed the game. I heard he was a seasoned vet and had already been in the NBA six years. Ron was 32 years old, tall, chocolate and fine. Just like I liked them. It didn't seem to bother him that I was barely 21. He called me, his "Lil' P.Y.T" - pretty young thing. The ho in me was ready to jump his bones and show him I could handle all 32 years of 'his' man.

After the game, we met Ron and his sister at the famous Isaac Hayes restaurant downtown Memphis. He was hospitable and made Danyeil feel comfortable and welcomed. His sister was super cool as well. She wasn't the prettiest, but she was Ron Taylor's little sister. That meant - she was excused. Her name was Kamya Taylor. She was short, high yellow with acne-infected skin. Her outfit took all the attention away from her ugly face. She had on the newest edition Ice Berg outfit with Goofy in sky blue. On her wrist, rested a fresh Rolex with the diamond bezel and two big ass diamonds in her ears, so being unattractive wasn't an issue. She kicked it with us like we had all went to high school together. It made me miss hanging out with my girls from high school, the "Classy Clique," as everybody called us. I guessed she was like that with all the girls her NBA brother tricked with. I didn't mind because tonight it was my turn. After eating and drinking we decided to call it a night. I was in bad need of an oil change and did not want to keep putting my car on the highway, so I borrowed my friend Candis' car for my over night rendezvous. I had to pay her to rent it for the night and plus, I had to fill up the gas tank. That was kosher 'cause I had to get back to this million-dollar nigga; I was trying to get on his team, with all intentions of being the star player. When we got back to Ron's house, his sister was already there. We chilled with her for about two hours, smoking and joking around. I was a bit skeptical about letting him know I smoked weed at first. I often hid this from male friends in fear that they would think less of me. But he made me feel so comfortable, I didn't even think twice about it. I hit the blunt and choked hard.

"Be careful, baby. That's not your average marijuana. That's hydro."

Hydro was the newest and stronger version of weed and it had a different blast to get you high. We smoked two hydro blunts and I was way gone. I don't even remember Kamya leaving. I was floating, zoned out. I felt like a straight up zombie. I couldn't think of a time I had been this high. The next thing I knew, Ron had his hands all over me. I thought this nigga turned into an octopus. I was so high. It felt like he had eight arms. Either that or he wasn't the only one touching me. He was rubbing, licking and massaging every part of me. My pussy was extra wet. I have never tried ecstasy, but I felt like he had laced my weed with it, although I knew he had not. That was just the feeling hydro gave you. He licked from my horizontal lips to my vertical ones. He devoured my pussy like it was his last supper. He had me reaching for the sky; he ate it so good. He knew exactly where the spot was to make me cum multiple times. He had my entire body shaking like I was having seizures. I don't know if it was the hydro or he was that damn good. All I kept thinking was, "Is this nigga gon' get the pussy and never call me no more, without me getting shit from him?"

I was extra horny from my pussy massage and I wanted so badly to ride that dick like a motorbike. He continued to suck my nipples and my belly. He was moaning like I was doing all the kissing. He kept mumbling, "Damn, I love your body. Damn, you fine!" He came face to face with me and tongued me down. I could taste my sweet juices in his mouth. I didn't care - it was mine. It wasn't like I was kissing him directly after he ate another bitch's pussy.

He whispered in my ear, "Are you ready for this?"

My lioness was screaming, *"Yes, tame me, Chaka!"*

My mind was thinking, *'hell no... you not about to fuck me and leave me alone.'* *My heart was thinking, 'no more pain, and no more drama.'* I decided to decline the dick offer, as badly as I wanted it. I figured if he wasn't going to call back, at least I had my pride and he didn't get to stick the pussy, only dipped his tongue in it. I got away with just giving him a sample of my golden brain (like that made me less of a ho in his eyes). When he finally busted, I laid back on the sofa, high as a kite, feeling like a straight up weedhead. Before I drifted off to sleep I prayed silently:

God please take this feeling away from me. I swear if I can make it through this night, I will never puff another blunt a day in my life. AMEN.

Chapter Thirty-Three

School was going well and my classes seemed to be too easy to be true. Or, I was just smarter than I thought. I changed my major to Sociology because it held my attention more than the others. We had lots of dumb papers to write. It seemed basically like we studied dumb-ass people and why they did dumb-ass things like dumb-ass crimes and other dumb-ass strange behaviors. It was interesting and I did find out a lot of things I didn't know and probably would have never known without those classes. I even thought I knew the solutions to half the problems plaguing my family. Some of them were just plain ole' crazy. They didn't have answers, just a bunch of excuses. My grades were looking good and I had a good relationship with all of my professors. I had given up cheerleading. Most of them had free admission to the, *"I hate Modesty club"* anyway, so that was a don data - a done deal. Sometimes females could be so caddy. Even I could be that way at times too.

❤ ❤ ❤ ❤ ❤

The day had finally come and Danyeil brought up the subject of her sorority. I tried to hide my anticipation. She asked me why I hadn't been to anyone's Rush, seeing as how the Diligent had just had theirs and the Zola and the Gamma's Rush was in less than a week. She knew I wasn't going to the Gamma or the Zola

Rush. Although, all the groups were constructive and prominent, everyone had their own stereotype of what kind of girls pledged certain sororities. The Zola's where often known to be tall, and unattractive or fat. I have to say; I'd met some pretty Zola's at other campuses that could fit other group stereotypes. Gammas were known to be the square unpopular girls, trying to fit in somewhere. The Diligent's were supposed to be the cool, ghetto and down to earth loud girls. Then there was the APG's, the pretty, light skin girls with long hair, often known to be snobs. This stereotyping reminded me of Spike Lee's movie, *School Daze*, where they had two sororities that reminded you of the Diligent and the APG's. Danyeil knew I wasn't going for Zola or Gamma. She didn't want to ask me about APG until the Diligent Rush had passed. She knew I was lively, very down to earth and at times ghetto, but at the same time I was light skin with a nice grade of hair and pretty. As tight as we had become, all she had to do was ask. She said she didn't ask 'cause she wanted to see what I would choose on my own and didn't want to seem manipulative. I assured her that she wouldn't alter my decision. I remember when she crossed; I watched their probate show in envy because I was supposed to cross with her. My grades were not up to par at the time, you needed at least a 2.5 and I only had a 2.3, so that year I missed my calling.

Danyeil invited me to meet her at one of her soror's house to hang out. But when I arrived, I knew she was up to something. Five of her other soror's that I recognized was there, plus two I had never seen before. They had invited other girls that I also knew from campus. To me, they seemed to be amongst some of the better-looking females on campus. All of the APG's introduced themselves one by one, with a cute greeting and their line name. When it was Danyeil's turn, she stood in front of all of us and recited:

"I'm pretty to my left, I'm pretty to my right, I'm so damn pretty, I can't sleep at night. Hi, I am AP-mosity, number 5 on my line of the 5 Divine Divas."

Each girl introduced herself by her line name. Then this tiny chic that called herself AP-teen, #1 of her line, told us why we were invited. She started off by saying, "Each of you may or may not know each other, but I would like each one of you to introduce yourself and state your classification and grade point." We each did this and looked at each other in pure inquisitiveness. "Today you have been hand picked to be a future APG woman in training. We will not beat you or force you to do obscene things against your will. We will not inflict any hurt, harm or danger in any way. All we want to do is overflow you with knowledge to prepare you to be amongst the best. Without any force, if you are willing to accept this offer step to the left. If you do not wish to participate, you may leave now and pretend this never happened and nothing will be held against you. There will be no hard feelings attached." Out of nine of us, two left. Those that were left looked at each other and shrugged our shoulders. I had no idea why they walked out, but I wasn't leaving to find out. The two that left were my square ass ex-neighbors of mine when I was in the dorms.

AP-teen told us we would need a pair of gray jogging pants and a white t-shirt that we had to wear every time we met. She also stated that nothing could be written down, but only memorized and never told to any one outside of the room. This was without a doubt a *secret society*. Then, AP-teen went on to state that if we hadn't already hung together, not to start. We were now considered L.S. (line sisters), but our actions and behaviors should not change, because if they did, it would be obvious that we were on line. When they asked if we had any questions, Shanya, a round dark chick raised her hand.

"Um, is this against campus rules or the sorority's rules or something?"

Danyeil spoke up. I mean, AP-mosity spoke up. "No, we're not hazing you; we're advancing your knowledge. Hazing is against campus rules as well as the sorority's rules. We are simply giving you a head start, which puts you at a lead over the other girls that will eventually join in March."

Then this chubby chick that they called AP-doit, spoke up. "You guys will learn things and know certain things that the others will not, which is a privilege to you. If you do not wish to have this benefit, you may leave now and never mention this night again."

Nobody left and the two girls who left earlier were never mentioned and they (to our knowledge) were never made mention of them, after that night. We found out that their reason for leaving though... pledging cost too much for them, took up to much time of their time and they thought it would interfere with their schooling. But for me, it helped my memory, attention span and loyalty to others. My big sisters became a part of me and possessed characteristics that I wanted to inherit. I truly felt the love we shared amongst each other and for the first time in my life I felt like I belonged to something with meaning... *positive* meaning at that. No longer was I involved with caddy ass females; these sistas were the 'real deal.'

Exactly ten weeks after that night. My six line sisters, including 10 other girls had a probate show in front of the student center. The seven of us were the closest. We held an unexplainable bond. Our entire line name was, *"The 17 Sisters of Sophistication."* The seven of us, unknowingly to others, carried our underground names over; I remained 'Stiletto', mainly because it was plain to see I would wear stilettos to the gym, if I could get away with it. My other soror's included: Silhouette, Silk, Shine, Sassy, Superior and Star Studded. We were all given our name based on our personalities and some actions during sessions. The remainder of my line sister's names also started with an, 'S' and fit our stylish theme. This was the night I had been looking forward to since the first night we all met up with Danyeil and the others. This was truly a milestone in my life, most definitely remarkable. I'd invited my family and closet friends from Milwaukee. This was truly a celebration, especially after all the long hard nights of secretly studying with my line sisters, surreptitiously exchanging notes and 'on the spot' pop quizzes. Oh, let's not for get all the late night and early morning 'errands' we were called to make. We had finally made it across the burning sands. Maraca, Mariah, Tracy B, Jurnee and several others cheered right in the front row as we marched towards the crowd, our arms and legs moving with precise motion. Our voices were loud and sharp, shouting our chants:

I love my A
I love my P
I love my APG
Epee gee, Epee gee
I tell no lie
I tell you why
I didn't pledge Diligent
Cuz I'm overqualified
I tell no lie
I tell the truth
I didn't pledge Zola
Cuz I'm to dayum cute
Oww! Oww! Owwww!

Everybody screamed in excited and awe. We each introduced our selves individually. A lot of people had it twisted. They'd mistaken all the stepping and partying for all fun and games. We had to labor for this name and to claim APG. We performed numerous amounts of community service, fundraisers, displayed leadership, as well as sisterhood, responsibility and commitment. I loved this whole sorority aura. New friends, new sisters and new experiences – that's what's up! All of this gave me a better approach and perspective on life. I will never forget the look on my niece's face when I performed in front of her. It made me feel swollen with pride. She stared up at me with complete admiration and I knew this had made a strong impression on her. I told her that one day she to could be an APG woman or apart of any Greek organization that she chooses, but only if she went to college and did well. We took so many pictures and I got lots of gifts. This was truly the best night of my life so far, and to think I wasn't going to go to college? Just the thought of not being a part of APG Sorority, Incorporated was unimaginable. It beat any gang association that I might have ended up joining, running around wild and loose at home. Tracy B gave me a congratulations card with a six-page letter inside. She and I had never really had a close relationship. Expressing feelings wasn't common in our household, so I guess the best way she knew how was to write a letter. She expressed her happiness for me and how proud she was of me. She even added a certificate to the mall. The woman loved her kids. She cracked jokes in the letter about her not paying the bills to come down to see me. It reminded me of when I was in high school.   She actually did skip important priorities to keep us happy with the latest designers. Tracy B. had honestly come a long way.   I remember there were times I couldn't tell if the young boys were parked outside of the house were for her, Maraca or me. Not anymore... she was now happily married to Wallie. She even said she mended ties with daddy and turned over his estate to my Aunt Kelly – what was left of it! Life was blessed for all of us. Maraca had gotten it together. She was expecting a baby boy with her fiancé, Skeeter. Even Austin managed to at least stay out of jail.   I was happy and so was my family. Society labeled us dysfunctional, but we were rising above the pressure and functioning. I had no objections. I couldn't ask for anything more at this point in my life; we were truly blessed.

❤ ❤ ❤ ❤ ❤

Ron Taylor and I had been involved for two months now and I had past made up for our first night together. We were now kicking it on a regular. He invited me to almost every game. He even bought me a living room set and paid to get my car fixed at one point. Not to mention, he sponsored my induction into the great APG women of fame. Things were fine with us, but not fine enough for me.   But, don't let his generosity fool you; times were not always smooth. There were times I wouldn't hear from him days at a time. He wasn't returning any of my phone calls, but what ended our courtship was when he stood me up for Valentine's Day.   I went out and spent my precious $150 on one of the sexiest gowns Victoria Secrets offered. I went to Spencer's and bought a box of scented rose pedals and a whole slew of candles. I bought him a card and a box of Curve cologne along with a throw off box of Old Spice. The card read, 'I love a man in Old Spice'. I bought the Old Spice as a joke to make him smile, since he joked about wearing it when we first met. We joked around a lot and that was one thing we liked about each other. We always keep one another smiling. I had asked Ron two weeks in advance to be my Valentine, so I just knew he would have me fabulous gift and a planned out night. Shit, that nigga didn't even answer his phone on Valentine's Day. I sent him text pages and called his phone off the hook, with no response from Mr. NBA. I didn't care who he was and what team he played for, Modesty Yameyeia Blair, was not going to be treated that way anymore! Valentine's day was just not a good holiday for me... for that, I don't celebrate that shit no more! Finally, two days later, Mr. NBA man wants to call me like he had no idea I had expected to spend that special day with him. His concocted story was his mother surprised him and brought his daughter from Chicago to spend the weekend with him. I knew it was a bullshit lie, but I didn't press the issue. I was trying to mature in many ways and calm down my wild and crazy temper. The old Modesty would have snapped out without thinking twice. I just accepted his apology and $1,000 dollars, and charged his inconsideration to the game. Shit, I had been done worst by that nigga JJ, Dillon and Skylar, so I couldn't complain – and they all supposedly loved me.

Ron T did help me mature sexually. He was one of those older niggas that was trying to turn a young woman out. We were into all type of kinky shit. He had me experimenting; doing things I never would have the gall too. I gave him all access to every part of my body. I didn't understand why a man would want to have anal sex. It reminded me of homosexuality, not to mention it started off as the worst pain one could inflict on another. It was okay after I got use to it, but initially, it literally tore my ass open. The only request I didn't grant is a threesome with another women. I probably would have, if I thought it would never get out. But even I know what happens in the dark always comes to light.

🕷 🕷 🕷 🕷 🕷

I was in Memphis like it was my second home. Danyeil and I had grown so close, while Jurnee and I barely saw each other or talked. Summer was coming into bloom and the semester was almost over. Jurnee was graduating this year from college with plans to move to Texas for medical school. That girl was truly my inspiration and she did not even know it. How many black kids do you know that are raised in broken homes with no expectations- whatsoever - make it as far as she has and will? And, she had it rough growing up. That goes to show nobody has to be a product of their environment, unless they choose to. Jurnee and I were not as close as we were in

225

high school, but I still had love for her and considered her more like a relative now, so with that I knew we would always be a part of each other lives.

Chapter Thirty-Four

This time instead of running home for the summer, I decided to do a little traveling. First I went to Memphis, of course and stayed a week with Danyeil and Ahmad, who were expecting their first child. I also stayed a few days with Ron T. He was scheduled to go back to Florida, since the season was over, so I had to get my visit in since I wasn't sure when I would see him again. I noticed a change in him and the interaction between us. I did a little extra begging since I knew the affair was basically over on Valentine's. Lastly, I went to ATL to kick it with my cousin, Chanel. She lived a fun and carefree life. Every time I saw her, she had something new happening in her world. We hung out like no tomorrow. She knew I was looking for a good time everytime I hit 'Hot-lanta'. We went to the Lenox Mall and balled out. I got a new Tiffany & CO. necklace and bracelet set. Of course I had to do what I did best. I lifted some designer rags for Chanel and myself from various stores. I was in lust when I saw the new line of bamboo purses Gucci had. I had to have one; I just needed a sponsor to buy it for me. It was no way I could afford a $900 purse and I still wasn't working. I called every nigga in my phone book, including this Nigerian dude named, Rauel Sawqua. I had just met the night before at club 112. Chanel thought it was funny that I asked him after just meeting him the night before, but shit all he could say was no and it wouldn't kill me... and if it ran him off, I didn't care. I didn't know his foreign ass like that, anyway! He took me to lunch at Justin's, Puff Daddy's restaurant in Georgia. While we waited on our dinner, I ran my mouthpiece, yapping about how hard it was being a college student. How much of a strain it was financially and all the nice things I wanted from the mall, but couldn't get because of my cash flow. I even went as far as telling him how bad I wanted the pocketbook. Just like I planned, he asked how much the purse was. I lied and said $1,800. He was a designer type of guy. Shit, his suit was Armani, so I knew the price wouldn't shake him. He offered to give me half and he did. Lord knows I could have done so much more with that money and did in fact need it, for so much more. But me, being me, I got that bamboo handle Gucci bag I yearned for. *"Black female addicted to retail, so irresponsible."* That's Modesty. I swear that song was written for me.

🏦 🏦 🏦 🏦 🏦

Chanel and I were cruising in her drop top Saab, when I got a call from Danyeil's number, only when I picked up it was Ahmad.

"Hey, Modesty. I was calling to tell you Danyeil lost the baby. If you can, it would be nice if you would come see her. I know how much she loves you and it would cheer her up a little. She's been so depressed since it happened."

I didn't know what to say since I knew how bad they wanted this baby and had been planning for her arrival. Danyeil was 7 months and they called it a miscarriage. Her baby was dead in her stomach and she still had to go through normal delivery.

"Ahmad, I am very sorry to hear that and if there is anything I can do, let me know. Also tell Danny I will be there early tomorrow morning." Chanel was disappointed that my stay was cut short, but she understood how close Danyeil and I was from the way I gabbed on about her.

When I got to Memphis I went straight to the hospital. When I walked into Danyeil's room, I could have fainted from what I saw. I thought this girl had wigged out. She was holding her dead baby, wrapped in a blanket, rocking and staring at the baby girl. She named her Chloe Yameyeia. I guess the trauma had her temporarily insane. I was lost for words; I mean what do you say at a time like this? Especially in the position she was in at this very moment – nothing. So, I just took a seat and waited for her to snap out of it. She didn't even look up at me. Not one time. Neither did she say anything. I stepped into the hallway and called Ahmad. Praying that he could give me the resolution to pep her up.

"Hey Ahmad, I'm at the hospital. Where are you?"

"Hey, Modesty. I had to go grab something to eat," he lied.

"What's up with, Danyeil? She's in the room holding the baby."

"I know she has been doing that since this morning. The doctor said she's in shock and it's okay for her to do it, if it helps her. I guess it's her self -therapy. Doc said they'll remove the baby soon." I had a puzzled look on my face and couldn't believe the hospital was allowing this.

"Well, she's not saying anything to me. Has she lost her sanity?"

Ahmad sighed, "It may seem like it, but she'll snap out of it. She's been going in and out all morning. I think it's the medicine that's contributing to her strange behaviors."

Before I could respond, a nursed walked up and told me I couldn't be on a cell phone in the hospital. So, I had to let Ahmad go.

"I gotta get off the phone, Ahmad. I'll see you when you get here."

"Modesty," he yelled before I hung up.

"What."

"Please stay with her. Please, hold her hand and comfort her. I don't know what else to do. She won't even talk to me. She's blaming me for the death of the baby."

I wanted so badly to ask what was going on and why was she blaming him? But this beastly looking ass nurse stood there until I hung up the phone. I sat with Danyeil for three hours and Ahmad hadn't called or come back to comfort her. Good thing Danyeil was asleep for two hours, but when she woke up, she started screamin' her head off because the baby was gone.

"Where is my baby, where the fuck is my baby girl?" I immediately ran to her side and held her hand. "Danyeil, it's okay sweetie. I'm here and Ahmad is on his way." I lied. She went into a rage. "Fuck Ahmad. Fuck everybody! I hate that son of a bitch. He killed my baby." I embraced her and wiped her weeping eyes. "Don't say that. God is going to take care of your baby, it's not anybody's fault. Nobody can control God's will." She cried harder. "No! God did not do this. Ahmad did! God punished him for it and punished me for not leaving Ahmad a long time ago." She cried hard, bitter tears (and I wept with my girl). I remained puzzled... 'cause I still didn't figure out what had transpired between them.

A couple days later, she was released from the hospital; it was to my surprise Ahmad hadn't come around. Now this was the same nigga living lavishly with her, but got ghost on her in the time of need. It was later explained by Danyeil that she told Ahmad to go home, back to Milwaukee and forget about what they had. The truth was, Ahmad had been cheating on her, and gave her and the baby an STD; along with all the stress of the relationship from all the fighting and arguing, those reasons caused their baby to die from a premature birth defect.

"That nigga could have given me AIDS. Then what? All of us would be having a funeral. He doesn't love me. He just loves that feeling he gets when that vein pops in his dick."

I sat there in shock, speechless. I always thought they had a perfect relationship. I didn't think of Ahmad that way. He appeared coy and madly in love with her. I always thought Danyeil was the best thing that ever happened to him. I guess you can't judge a book by its cover. Niggas do grimy things regardless of their stelo, square or hood; a dog will be a dog in spite of its exterior.

"But Danyeil, how can you say it's over like that after all those years of being with him? ... I mean you were out there too. We all make mistakes."

She responded, "It's either that nigga or my life. Fuck 'em! 'Cause I refuse to ever love flesh more than I love myself or my God." Her point was valid! I totally agreed with that, but I knew as well as she did, it wouldn't be that easy to walk away from him. It only reminded me that what we love so much could sometimes be the worst thing for us. Damn Danyeil and Ahmad! I hope shit works out for y'all.

Chapter Thirty-Five

Senior year, the year I had been waiting for! *Please believe it!* My advisor set me up with the local boy's group home for an internship in exchange for 3 credit hours. I was also working part-time at a day care center. My income was considered poverty, so rent assistance lowered my rent down to $150 monthly. Everything was good for me. Now my only downfall was the fact that I was all into my feelings for Ron T and he wasn't thinking about my ass. I called him every chance I got and 75% of the time he ignored me. If Florida weren't as far, I probably would have been at his doorstep. My love life on campus was non-existent – basically over. I had to make one of these younglings my new 'boy toy' and fast. I finally gave up the thought of Ron T and realized it was good while it lasted. Realistically, we never could have been an item. It was rumored he had a wife back in Florida anyway. With my luck, I knew it was most likely true!

Sticky fingers took it down a notch; I still shoplifted occasionally, but I slowed down since people were getting caught at the local mall left and right. Not excluding the fact that Jaysa and her 'gym-shoe' crew kept spreading gossip about me. It didn't bother me as much because I knew what the real was. It was in my blood, in my nature to be a Diva. My daddy started that at birth, so I didn't waste a brain cell thinking about

Jaysa's malicious attempts. Most people ignored her anyway because they knew she had it out for me, but the ho disliked me in everyway. It's like we were rivals in every aspect. I pledged APG... she pledged Diligent. I ran for homecoming queen... so did she. I moved off campus to a low budget apartment... she moved off campus to a nice complex. I mean the list goes on and on and on. It was foolish 'cause she smiled and talked to me like I didn't know she internally despised me. Everybody knew the feeling was mutual, but we remained cordial, frontin' like it was all-good, knowing it wasn't.

With homecoming impending I had to get my gear tight, as usual. So me, Savanna and Corrine drove to Nashville to go to one of their best malls. With Corrine all up in my groove, stealing me a new outfit was almost impossible. That girl was an irritating shadow. Everything I picked up she was watching. Or, when I went in with something she made sure she asked about it when I came out. I figured she was suspicious 'cause back in the day, when we were roommates, I stole the exact outfit she had purchased and knew she left the receipt in the bag. I took her receipt along with my stolen outfit, back and got refunded the money. I had to break free to get my five-finger on. So, I dipped away from her to get down to business. Eventually, we lost Corrine in on of the stores and got down to business.

🕷 🕷 🕷 🕷 🕷

Homecoming was all of that! However, I didn't win homecoming queen, but neither did Jaysa. I was first runner up and Jaysa, to my delight, was second runner up. This year I was not only part of a Greek organization, I was eligible to participate with all of the events they did for homecoming. The step show was one of my favorites. All of the Greek organizations competed for the step shows best title. As usual, the Red dudes took the title for the boys and of course the APG's, for the girls. I was also a part of the homecoming court. For one, because I was first runner up for homecoming queen, and two: I had won the 'Ms. Black and Gold' pageant back in September, so I had to represent for my frat brothers of Black and Gold. The homecoming party was off the chain. I was in search for this fine dark Hershey kiss I peeped at the step show. I noticed him when the Dogs, (one of the fraternities) did their thing. He was a Dog and he looked PHAT (pretty hot and tempting)... his dog collar yoked around his neck, with the chain hanging low. It brought attention to his large dick print showing through his army fatigue pants. I inquired about him and found out his name, Kendal "Buck Wild", #4 of his line. I wanted Kendal to come home with me and get buck wild at "Chez Modesty". I had to let the ho in me out for my last for homecoming weekend as a college student. When I saw him at the party, I made sure I was in his eyesight. When I caught him looking, I started dancing really sexy and provocative. I had on some fitted Fendi logo pants and a shirt that only covered my ta-tas, with a thin string that held it together in the back. And of course, when I hypnotized him with my hips - he was mine. He came over and we danced to *'Wait,'* by the *Ying Yang Twins*. I made sure he felt every curve of my body and saw the sextrastion (sexual frustration) in my eyes. I started kissing his sweaty neck and rolling my tongue across his ear lobe. Yes, salty and all. His moans turned me on. And, guess what? We hadn't even exchanged names yet, but I already knew his.

I whispered seductively in his ear, "By the way, I'm Modesty."

"I know Ms. Stiletto, and I am Kendal."

"Oh, I know... aka, Mr. Buck Wild."

Hell yeah, it was on from there! He knew of me and I knew of him. We continued molesting each other on the dance floor. The night ended with him in my bed, my living room, my kitchen and my bathroom. The buzz, was right it, ...ain't nothing like a Dog... those nasty, nasty barkin' Dogs! *Ooooowwww!*

Chapter Thirty-Six

With graduation just two months away, I had already started preparing. I mailed out invitations to almost every known address in Milwaukee: family, enemies, friends and friendemies. Even those I knew on lock down and restriction. (Like they could really make it.) I wanted mothafuckas to know... me, – Modesty Yameyeia Blair, was graduating from college. Even JJ phoned from prison to tell me congratulations. He had his cellmate draw me a congratulations card, with some of his jailhouse photos enclosed. He had already been in jail damn near the past year. He got caught up in some robbery shit with his wild ass little brother, Lil' Boy. He had three more long years to go. But who was counting? Not me. After all those years of addiction to his ass, when they told me he got locked up, I had a chance to detoxify from him. Sad, but true... I knew it was no way in hell I could relapse after I had been rehabilitated. 'Miss Stiletto Princess' wasn't strutting in any damn prison for nobody, not even JJ. I had finally shuck that bad habit, the dependency of the "JJ's". It seems crazy when I think about, how much mind-control that man had over me. And to be honest, I think it was more of him going to jail that allowed room for me to get over him, rather than all the hurt and pain he caused me for so many years. I guess that proves my theory true, *'out of sight, out of mind'*. That may sound fucked up, but I look at like this… I did four years in college with no help, support… nothing from him. He could have sent some money, stamps… shit something to help hold me down, when I was in need. I hope he don't think I'm supposed to look out with commissary for him… I don't think so! He better holla at all them ho's, *pimpin'*. I too, promised myself to never again love a man more than I loved God or myself. It's a shame how half these nigga take a good woman for granted. They'd rather have a hood rat with several kids, several baby daddies, no long-term goals and collecting welfare; rather than a woman with a bright future… even if she were a reformed ho. I had a lot to look forward to. I was about to graduate from college with many options now available – almost ready to meet the future.

One of my soror sister's had approached me about a job (that was surely a sorority perk – having connections), but I was still undecided if I wanted to relocate, or go back to Milwaukee. I think my heart desired more to relocate. I just wished I could take my family with me. I knew Tracy B and Maraca wasn't even trying to hear that. They were both content and didn't like change as much as I had grown accustomed too.

Being away for college really broadened my horizons. If I would have never left, I can't imagine what would have become of me. Imagine that??? I mean being away - I traveled, met all kind of interesting people – famous – professional – resourceful, had a chance to live college campus life and experience life for myself. Not saying that people of this stature didn't exist at home, but if I hadn't left Milwaukee and gone away to college, I would have been complacent like so many teenagers there. Previously my idea of going out of town was the Wisconsin Dells. A large, popular water resort, about an hour and half away from Milwaukee. But these days, I was in a different state almost every other weekend with no hesitation. I sat and thought about all the good times I had at Lane College and I sort of wished this last year could be extended. Thanks to Lane's summer classes, even Savanna was graduating college this year.

♥ ♥ ♥ ♥ ♥

I've always been a firm believer in, where there is good - bad is not far behind. My sister's phone call brought good and bad together. Maraca called to tell me she gave birth to a 7lb baby boy, named Malik Shabbaz. She and Skeeter were studying the Muslim religion. He now called himself, Shabazz. I teased her on what her Muslim name would be and how she would have to wear sheets instead of regular clothing. She corrected me that they weren't sheets, but considered Muslim Garb. I was proud of her new transformation. She also told me of some very disturbing news. Linda, my old running partner, was found dead in her own apartment the same night my sister gave birth. There's an old saying, 'with every death new life is born.' Linda was killed by an undercover, functioning psychotic trick. She was on a date for money and the guy wanted to do things she didn't agree with. He raped and killed her in rage. He was a high school principal, with wa-a-ay too many secrets in his closet. He was convicted of 1st degree murder and rape. The worst part about it, he was only given 5 years in prison and 5 years on probation because the officials claimed the murder was in self-defense. He claimed she tried to rob him. Using her own weapon against her, a pearl handle 22' (my Peggy Sue pearl handle that she had stolen out of my crib when I thought I misplaced it), he shot her once in the head. His good reputation and education got him a major time cut. That's real fucked up how a person can murder someone and get a slap on the wrist, but you can get indicted on drug charges or conspiracy and get ten to life. Where's the justice? That alone made me thank God for His act in my life. I had put myself in many situations that only God knew how to get me out of, and thankfully I came out of them alive. So, hearing this news saddened me. Not only for her death, but because it was my weapon that put her under. Damn, I felt fucked up! RIP Linda, I love you girl no matter how shit turned out for us!

I sat back and thought about a similar situation I was in. I never told a soul to this day. It was this guy name Shecar; I met him by way of Savanna. To keep it real, he was a guy that Savanna used to fuck on in high school, periodically. Every time I would come home for college breaks, he was at me. Always trying his hardest to get me to holla at him. At first, I keep rejecting him. Then I gave in, allowing his material wealth to impress me. I know I was wrong for going behind my girl, but I felt like I owed her one anyway for those times she did not have my back. I also felt like, what she didn't know, wouldn't hurt and I fed my lust. The next time I saw dude at the mall, I gave signs that I was 'bout it. I was on a mission looking for a pair of stilettos to wear to this party that was going down at a new club called, The Matrix. Somebody covered my eyes from behind, it just so happened to be Shecar.

"What's up, Shecar?" I said as I turned around to greet him. I couldn't help but notice his Presidential Rolex and diamond filled necklace.

"Hey, Modesty. I see you still looking good. You ready for me yet?" He flashed his diamond filled, platinum teeth.

"Boy, please...stop it." I hit his arm playfully.

"Stop what? I like you; I've always liked you, but you so full of it. You the one gon' miss out, though. So, I'll let you go back to yo' little shopping. I know you going out tonight. So, I'll check you later." As he was about to walk away, he stopped and asked, "How long you been in this mall?"

I replied, "About an hour or more. Why?"

He had a sinister grin on his face. "Because I know your taste. You're high maintenance and this mall don't have nothing for your speed. Why don't you roll to Chicago with me and we can hit Michigan Street? I got you."

Those were the magic words. I was hypnotized. How could I refuse the offer? With two snaps and a twist, I was ready to roll. Before we hit the highway he had to slide the, "are you staying with me tonight", comment in there. I agreed, (of course) 'cause I wanted to go shopping on *him*. We drove to this mall right outside of Chicago instead, called Old Orchard. We only hit like four stores before he was ready to call it quits. I managed to get a pair of signature Louis Vutton sandals on him. Before we headed home, we stopped and ate at The Cheese Cake Factory. He started the conversation off with, "You know I got to be feeling you to spend almost $400 dollars on some punk ass sandals. I don't usually do that." He stared at me, waiting on a response. I was a little flattered; it was big for this cheap ass nigga, 'cause I know Savanna barely got dinner and a movie out of this him, which was the minimum that I required. Here I was with the newest 'Loui' signature sandals, fresh off the shelf. So, I made plans to trick with him for the night (it was a sleazy call, I know) after the club. He picked me up in his clean Infiniti Q 45. It smelled so good inside, like fresh leather. The seats felt soft and comfortable. I relaxed and inhaled the scent of the new car air freshener. It reminded me of how Daddy's BMW, used to smell. I was chill until we drove off to an unknown location, not where we intended to rest.

"Thanks for everything today. I had a good time and I love my shoes."

"Aw, baby its nothing. If you fucks with me, it gets better than that." Don't all niggas run this line? I rolled my eyes back and let him continue, "That's just the beginning of how good things would be for you. And besides, I don't care what nobody says, we all trick for what we strongly desire. If a bitch or a nigga say that they haven't, they some lying mothafuckas!"

I gave a fake smile. I felt a little uncomfortable because I was about to share a dick with one of my closest friends on the strength that the nigga bought me Loui sandals. I felt terrible. Thinking to myself, I decided before we parked, I wasn't goin' play myself like no prostitute regardless of what his philosophy was. There had been many times that I'd laid next to a man without having sex. Hopefully, playing with the pussy for him would be good enough. A good tease doesn't hurt... at least that's what I thought.

When we pulled up to the block that appeared to be 'Crackhead Ave' I knew then, he was treating me like a sure-bred tramp. We walked in the heavy traffic having spot and entered the main room. It had a full size bed pushed against the wall in what I thought was the living room, sitting on crates, with a small 13" television also sitting on a crate. That alone was a turnoff, and I definitely wasn't feelin' this shit. That went out of style back in high school... fucking in dope spots. What happened to him thinking I was so high maintenance? He read the expression on my face and tried to run script.

"Ahh, baby. This one of the houses I just bought. I haven't decided if I'm gonna rent it out or not. So I just use it as my honeycomb hideout for now."

I wanted to 100-yard dash out that bitch! He gave me his tee shirt to sleep in and he slept in his boxers. As soon as we lay down, he was all over me.

"I heard you got some good, wet pussy," he whispered in my ear. I didn't say a damn thing. I wasn't trying to get this aggressive negro hard. He started rubbing my ass and thighs. He was breathing so heavy, sounding like a maniac. I tried to distract him, so (dumb ass me) asked him to give me a massage. Wrong move! That was the wrong request 'cause he immediately asked me to remove the oversized tee shirt. Before I knew it, his fingers were digging in and out of my intimate spot, roughly. I asked him to stop, but he just went faster. He demanded for me to take off my panties. I refused; that's when he let the beast out. He ripped off my only pair of La Pearla underwear like a piece of paper. My heart started thumping so hard, he probably heard it.

"Why you playing hard to get? You know you want this big dick. Man, niggas know that you a ho. Why you gon' front on me? What? I ain't good enough to get the pussy?" Shecar's tone was harsh and the look on his face made it distorted. The demon in him came out of hiding.

"Please, don't do this Shecar. You're drunk and high... and you're hurting me! Please stop," I pleaded with him. This only made him angrier.

He held me down by the neck and my body grew very tense from fear. With his other hand, he jammed his dry dick inside of me, pumping harder and deeper, with as much force as his intoxicated body would allow.

"Your little flirty-ass been asking for this all day. You know you want this. I know I'm worth this pussy. I ain't got to beg for this pussy... I paid for this shit! I bought you those expensive ass shoes; you better give me this shit... throw that pussy back!" He carried on a conversation with himself the whole time. I didn't respond to anything he said. I just lay there stiff and fearful, being violated. This dude had taken the pussy – date rape is the official term for what he had done. I was afraid to move as burning tears ran into both my ears. I couldn't believe I was being raped...degraded by someone I knew personally. After the horror, he fell asleep ontop of me snoring. I just lay there too sore and frightened to move. I didn't want to wake him and have him start all over again to have his way again with my body. I should have ran out, listened to my better judgment – that little voice that warned me against him, but my desire for material things had me jammed up. I silently blamed myself for this. I shouldn't have been acting like a ho. So, I never had him prosecuted – too ashamed I guess. How was I going to prove my case in court? I prayed to God in my head to protect me through the night and return me home in one piece.

The next morning he got up like nothing happened. He told me to hurry and shower, so he could take me home. I wanted to get in the shower when I got home, but he insisted I take one there. That probably was for me to wash the evidence away. On the way home all I could think about was last night's nightmare. We rode all the way to my house with the radio blastin' as loud as the volume would go. His music was so loud I couldn't even think. I didn't want to look his way. I hated his guts for what he did to me. I felt like it was practically my fault because I should have never fucked with him in the first place, I never should have went home with him after the club and I definitely shouldn't let him think what he did last night was okay. I mean, I see commercials all the time, "NO MEANS NO!" regardless of what else. And, there I was blaming myself and not admitting he violated me to anyone else. I had to tell it to someone, so here I am pouring my hurt out to the world. Not for sympathy, but to finally get it off my chest!

As soon as he hit the corner to my house, my hand was on the door handle. Before I could jump out of the half moving car, he grabbed my arm.

"You got a few scratches on your neck. What are you going to say happened?" he asked in a casual tone.

"I don't know." Avoiding eye contact, I stared away out the window with a look of disgust.

"Well, I'd hate for you to claim rape, when you asked for it. I know you smarter than that? And besides if you did, I got money for the best lawyers in the city. That would be a *long* and tedious battle. I'll have niggas lined up for days testifying how easy you are. I know you ain't that stupid. Besides, you know I didn't mean to hurt you. I was drunk and you were acting like a little tease. How you gon' try and play a nigga like that... asking for a massage and shit, showing off yo' lil' ass, then wanna play innocent."

My eyes started to burn from trying to hold back my tears. "I'm straight. You don't have to worry about me." I walked in the house humiliated and degraded, slamming the door on that scene in my life. I vowed never to put myself in that predicament ever again, and I never told anybody. I heard he mentioned to someone, he fucked me. I denied it and blocked that night out of my head. But guess what? I also heard he was presently serving time for raping an under-aged girl. If I would have told, it may have prevented the next female from getting raped. God, I'm sorry I didn't... but now, getting sodomized by a homo-thug is his biggest worry! What comes around goes around... and not even his money could save that ass now. Trick ass mark! Who's laughing now?

✦ ✦ ✦ ✦ ✦

There was so many signs telling me don't move back home. I had many good memories, but even more bad ones. There was a huge indictment in Milwaukee; it was full of murders and drug dealers – a new crew of guys known as the Ghetto Mafia, and the other, the Murk Mob. It was said that they had involvement in most of the cities unsolved murders, dated all the way back! Some of the members were labeled drug kingpins, contracted assassinators or just by mere association. Included in this big city wide bust were more than a few that I knew. All I could think of was, "Damn, it ain't gone be no good niggas to fuck wit' when I get home." That was an ignorant remark and even I knew I was wrong for thinking that. Family's lost their loved ones to the system and here I was thinking about who's left to fuck wit'. That was weak of me. My soror sisters always pulled me up on this type of behavior, but it had to be in me to change. I think I'm ready to take them up on that. That alone proved I still had some ill manners to deal with. It would be a hard fight, but I was going to contain that wild side. Even, when I began my career in the corporate world. Don't let those uppity chicks wearing stilettos fool you; they all have a little ho in them. My next thought was thank God, I was given a chance to step outside the box. APG Sorority, Inc. was my pivotal point at Lane College. I may have been raised in the bowels of society, but Lane College and the sister love of APG. Sorority, Inc. snatched me up out of that fire. Often times I think of Linda, regretting the fact that the streets had taken her under and how we let petty shit come between us. She was my dawg – one of my partna's in crime! We did dirt together... I miss her to death (even though we had our times) and wished I could've saved her from becoming a victim of urban manipulation.

True... I was from the ghetto, designed to hold me down, and labeled an underdog by society - but I out ran that bitch... jumping over all of it's hurdles: drugs, alcohol, government induced dysfunctional homes, street gangs, night hustles, jail, dirty fights, unwanted pregnancies, dropping out of school... and let's not forget my weakness for a no-good chocolate thug. I soared above it all with the empowerment and support of an education from a HBCU and above all... the love and support of my APG sorors. I felt like returning home would be a mistake... like I would be returning to destruction. But I guess things will only happen if I allowed them. My thoughts were twisted... I was perplexed. I wanted to be with my family and my true home girls. But on the other hand, I wanted to stay down south. I guess I would cross that bridge when it was time. Being away from home, revealed my self-discovery and a *"mature"* Modesty. I was a part of something that really mattered, APG Sorority, Inc. I was doing what I knew grandma always wanted. I was going to church not frequently, but it was a start. You can't change overnight; it's a slow process. At least I was working on the spiritual part of my life. My previous prayers were, "God, please protect me from my enemies and allow me to see another day." Now I prayed, "God, thank You for Your many blessings; please continue to order my steps."

Danyeil was petitioning me to move to Memphis with her. I was lost, so I left it up to God to decide. I prayed about it and didn't let it worry me anymore. Wherever I ended up living, I felt it was meant to be... it was in HIS book.

Chapter Thirty-Seven

I was handling my final college affairs. I had to complete all the necessary paperwork for graduation: graduation application, senior fees, my cap and gown fitting and most importantly - the senior exit exams. And of course, this story wouldn't end right if I didn't have any exit drama. It was the senior barbeque at Muse Park and almost all of LC was there. It was crackin' so hard. I was so amped because I was one of the reasons for this 'senior' shindig. I was proud of my accomplishments. It reminded me of the big Father's Day barbeque the men from home used to throw. The next scene definitely reminded me of something that would occur at home. Jaysa waddled her 8-month fat, pregnant-ass in my face with some last-day-of-school bullshit, like in elementary school or something.

"Modesty, you telling people I don't know who my baby daddy is?" She just wanted a reason to fight.

I calmly replied, *"Guuurl, pul-leaze*... ask me if I care." She was determined to turn it into an argument anyway.

"Don't get smart!"

Now, the old Modesty would have been ready to get in her ass. I would have pulled one of my "your face ain't pregnant" moves and got down. But I was not the same person. I had more to lose because I had something to stand for. She had been asking me to put hands on her for 3 years now. So I thought rationally. Everything I did from this moment on would affect my future. I wasn't about to be unemployed for checking 'yes' on the box that asks, *"Have you ever been convicted of a felony?"* In my early stages, I probably wouldn't care, but now it was different. I was tired of fighting over a damn man! That shit had become real old to me. I knew if I hit that tramp, all my anger would lash out from the past years and I would have an attempted murder charge for damn near killing that ho'. I took a deep breath and replied maturely.

"I'm not getting smart, Jaysa. It's all-good. Congratulations on your new baby and good luck with your graduation next year... *FAREWELL.*" I had finally got a chance to use what the high school guidance counselor used on me – ironic, Pig Latin. I knew she felt stupid and exposed. I had already checked the senior's graduating list at the college registrar's office, only to find out that her name wasn't listed. I let her feel like she had bragging rights to say I punked out. I didn't care. She already had more than she could handle, she didn't need an ass whopping added on. I turned and walked away, leaving her in my past. She stood there speechless and dumbfounded, staring at the words on the back of my sorority t-shirt. In big pink letters it read: **STILETTO 101: DON'T LET THE STILETTOS FOOL YOU...**

❖ ❖ ❖ ❖ ❖

It's four days before graduation and I'm sitting, filling out my senior clearance forms with a huge Colgate smile on my face. This single sheet of paper is the last fling I'll have with this college before I walked across that stage profiling my famous Miss America wave and shake hands with the president of the school. It was a helluva' struggle, but I came out 'one-two' stepping in my stilettos. Who would have known I would have graduated from college on time, *exactly* four years after high school? Yeah, So Mr. Lynn, my high school counselor can kiss my 'educated' pretty ass. Instead of guiding and advising me to college, he gave me a farewell to welfare and jail – asshole. But, I'll have to admit, I surprised my damn self... I had one last thing to do – write my daddy to tell him I did it! He would be proud to know his 'daddy's girl' finally evolved into a woman.

This is the close of this chapter in my life, but not the end of Modesty Yameyeia Blair.

P.S. *In life there are no guarantees, but with GOD, there are no limits.*

It's ya girl,
Modesty Yameyeia Blair

Precioustymes Entertainment
New Releases Coming Soon!

Latin Heat by BP Love

At The Courts Mercy by KaShamba Williams

Mind Games by KaShamba Williams

Vendetta – Diary of a Kingpin's daughter by
Lenaise Meyeil

Hittin' Numbers by Unique J. Shannon

Dirty Dawg by Unique J. Shannon

www.precioustymes.com

Titles by
KaShamba Williams

Platinum Teen Series
(For 10 –15 year olds)
Book One – Dymond In The Rough

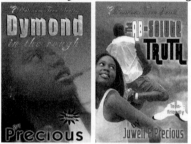

Book two coming July ... The 'AB'-solute Truth
Exclusively for your preteen/teen!!

QTY	TITLE	PRICE
	At The Courts Mercy by KaShamba Williams	$14.95
	DRIVEN by KaShamba Williams	$14.95
	Dirty Dawg by Unique J. Shannon	$14.95
	Hittin' Numbers by Unique J. Shannon	$14.95
	Latin Heat by BP Love	$14.95
	Mind Games by KaShamba Williams	$14.95
	Stiletto 101 by Lenaise Meyeil	$14.95
	Vendetta – by Lenaise Meyeil	$14.95
	PLATINUM TEEN SERIES	
	Dymond In The Rough	$6.99
	The AB-solute Truth	$6.99
	Total:	

Please include shipping and handling fee of $2.50.
Forms of payment accepted – money orders, credit card,
Paypal, debit cards, postal stamps and Institutional checks.
Please allow 5-7 business days for books to arrive.